CW00796612

High Jump

The girl got out of the yellow sports Jag and walked towards the Arrow Bridge.

Walked straight into the messed-up lives of Bogan, the maverick street cop who bends the law to suit himself; Nigel, his new partner, an eager young graduate—and Vicky Rivers, a firebrand internal police investigator out to prove herself in a man's world.

As the girl climbs the bridge, a tense police drama unfolds. Can the officers involved come to terms with their own frailties as they race against time to unlock the mystery of the girl on the bridge and solve the hide-and-seek riddle of her disappearing Jaguar?

Or, on that fateful day when the city holds its breath, are they all for the high jump?

by the same author

CRACKSHOT
SNOW MAN
THE HUNTER
GARVEY'S CODE
NEW FACE IN HELL
PATTERN OF VIOLENCE
A REASONABLE MAN
DEADLOCK
THE FRIGHTENERS
ROBBERY BLUE

ROGER BUSBY

High Jump

THE CRIME CLUB
An Imprint of HarperCollins *Publishers*

First published in Great Britain in 1992
by The Crime Club, an imprint of
HarperCollins Publishers, 77–85 Fulham Palace Road,
Hammersmith, London W6 8JB

9 8 7 6 5 4 3 2 1

A catalogue record for this book is
available from the British Library

ISBN 0 00 232390 7

Photoset in Linotron Baskerville by
Rowland Phototypesetting Ltd
Bury St Edmunds, Suffolk
Printed and bound in Great Britain by
HarperCollins Book Manufacturing, Glasgow

For Maureen

CHAPTER 1

Jojo drove the canary yellow XJS convertible into the lay-by on the bridge approach, rolled slowly down the white herringbone painted on the tarmac, turned into the furthest slot facing the guard rail, set the selector in park and applied the handbrake. She leaned back against the head-rest and closed her eyes as The Doors teased 'Stoned Immaculate' from the eight-track stereo, the music swirling around inside the Jaguar. On the dying notes she opened her eyes, killed the engine, took the key from the ignition and got out of the car.

It was early morning on a bright spring day, but the warmth of the sun striking the windshield had been deceptive for now she felt the bite of the chill breeze as she walked across to the guard rail and looked out on the clean inverted arc of the bridge spanning the gorge above the river far below. She had on a turquoise shell suit and white kickers, her blonde hair held back in a ponytail. As usual, she wore minimal make-up, just a little powder and lipstick which gave her light tan a translucent glow. Her mouth was a little too wide, her nose a trifle too long for the fashion pages, and it was left to the innocent blue of her eyes to create that special appeal in her face. She leaned on the rail and stared at the bridge.

'Pretty as a picture.' A man's voice behind her made her turn suddenly, startled. He wore an anorak over some kind of uniform and was carrying a canvas satchel.

'You're a real beauty.' He whistled in admiration and her first instinctive reaction, that this was some kind of clumsy pick-up, vanished as she realized his attention was not on her, but on the XJS. Now that she looked at him more closely, she could see that he was middle-aged with thinning hair and old-fashioned gold-rimmed glasses.

'I always loved you big cats.' He kept on talking to the Jaguar which responded with the rasping metallic purr of the cooling engine. 'Not that I ever owned one myself, you understand, never had that kind of money, but I did have a rag-top once, back in the 'sixties, Vitesse convertible, straight six, went like smoke.' He looked at Jojo for the first time, the memory lighting up his face. 'Young and crazy. Oh, I loved that car, they don't make 'em like that any more. Just tin cans now, sixteen-valve this, turbo-charged that, all the same.' He glanced quickly at the Jaguar, a pained expression flashing across his brow as though his comment might have offended. 'All except the big cats, of course, they've always kept the mystique. I bet this beauty handles sweet as a lover's kiss . . .' His cheeks coloured and he looked embarrassed. 'Oh, I'm sorry, didn't mean to be personal. I just got carried away.'

'It's OK,' Jojo said. 'I just . . . I never thought about it like that. It's my boyfriend's car. One thing you can bank on with Michael, he likes 'em sleek and fast.' She bit her lip at the catch in her voice, talking to a stranger like that, exposing a raw nerve. Not that the man had noticed. He was back in his dreams, blasting a works E-Type around Brooklands.

'Classical lines,' the man said. 'Like that bridge there. Not just functional, but easy on the eye, do the job with a little bit of magic. That's what sets 'em apart from the rest. You interested in bridges?'

She looked at the bridge. 'I always wondered. Why did they call it the Arrow Bridge?'

'Ah, that's just it. See the towers there?' He pointed. 'They go five hundred feet above the water just to get the angle on the cables right. Now you half close your eyes and look at the top of the towers where the cables come off and you could swear you're looking at arrowheads. It was designed that way, so there's no other name for it. Had to be the Arrow Bridge.'

'You seem to know a lot about it?'

'I ought to. I work on the tolls. I sit in that booth there all day with my hand out taking a quid off every car crosses over. Most of 'em don't even look up, don't even know what they're missing. Ask me about poetry, I'll tell you about that bridge.' He shrugged. 'I dunno what it is, some things you know are just right the minute you look at them, this cat of yours, that bridge.'

Jojo returned his tentative smile. 'I suppose if you do a job like that, you'd go out of your mind if you didn't have some purpose to it, something worthwhile.'

'You can say that again. Some of the guys, some of 'em just see it as boring work, you know? Grab what you can, fiddle the machines, pocket the proceeds. They don't understand.'

Jojo chuckled. 'Sounds to me as if you and that bridge have got something going.'

The man blushed. 'Now that's something I never thought of. You ought to tell my missus that, she'd split her sides. But we've had our moments, me and that bridge. We've had all sorts of maniacs. See the towers there? There's a ladder goes up the outside, for the maintenance crews, like climbing clear into the sky. We've had 'em up there, when we first opened, the Jesus freaks, screaming the end of the world. Then the bungees were all the rage. They'd sneak on to the span with a rubber rope in their rucksacks, hitch on to a girder and jump over the side. Just before they hit the water the bungee'd yank 'em back up. Got to have a screw loose to get your kicks doing a stunt like that.'

The man looked at his watch, saw it was 7.55. He hitched his satchel over his shoulder. 'Well, I'd better get going, time to clock on the shift.' He looked a little puzzled, perplexed by his own behaviour. 'Look,' he apologized earnestly, 'I hope you don't mind me bending your ear like this.

You being alone up here, I should've realized, you might get the wrong idea.'

'It's OK,' she said. 'I already got the feeling that you're a perfect gentleman.'

He gave her a little bow. 'Not many of us left, eh? Well, you take care now—' he nodded towards the Jaguar—'and take care of that baby too, I wouldn't want any harm to come to either one of you.' The man began to walk down the approach road towards the bridge with a jaunty step. When he was some distance away he turned and called back, struck by an afterthought, 'Hey, next time you're coming over the bridge, take lane two, that's my booth, and give me a smile for good luck.'

Jojo waved her hand, but she was already thinking about something else. She squinted at the sun, an orange ball, low down, clearing the morning haze, and then leaned on the rail and looked down at the river way below, the breeze stirring the water in perfect symmetry, like hammered pewter, the neck of the gorge opening out to the estuary and the Navy dockyard where grey hulks of warships huddled under the wings of the cranes. She was thinking about Michael and the good times they'd had when they first met. He'd been in the Navy then, a clearance diver finishing his hitch as an instructor at the diving school. If she screwed up her eyes against the glare she could just make out the clutch of low buildings jutting out into the deep water channel beyond the shipyard. That was where he'd taught her underwater swimming in the grey puddle of the training tank, looking like some exotic sea creature in her coral-coloured bikini. He'd shown her tricks with the snorkel and air tanks, and when she was good enough, he'd taken her skinny-dipping off the pontoon and had taught her buddy-breathing, going down deep with one tank between them, taking turns on the air line. In the green shadowy depths, he would take in air and then put his mouth to hers and let her breathe from his lips. They made love underwater, locked together like a pair of playful dolphins, and she saw the glitter in his eyes and misread the signs.

When he came out of the Navy, Michael had set up for himself doing the only thing he knew well enough to turn his hand to, teaching underwater swimming and making a good living off the tourists during the season, taking them down deep for a taste of the ultimate thrill. She was living with him then, buying their own flat in a shoreline development overlooking the marina, working as a negotiator for an estate agent and making a packet on commission during the boom years when the status symbol was a luxury apartment with balcony and sea views which had to be had no matter what the cost. Those were the good times.

From her vantage-point Jojo could make out the crescent of the apartment block on the far side of the river, the white concrete catching the sun, the neat lines of pleasure boats moored to the pontoons inside the artificial harbour of the Dolphin Marina like a miniature floating village. She stood there for a while until the brightness from the rising sun glinting off the water hurt her eyes and she turned and walked the dozen paces back to the Jaguar and opened the driver's door. She eased herself into the soft cream hide of the seat and blinked in surprise as she saw the knife lying on the rubber footmat set into the beige Wilton which ran down the tunnel to the pedals. It was a diver's knife with a black plastic handle and a straight blade serrated along one edge. The blade was heavily bloodstained. Jojo caught her breath, a flutter of panic constricting her throat. Carefully, with the toe of her trainer, she kicked the knife out of sight under the seat.

CHAPTER 2

Bogan awoke the instant he heard the sound. He lay perfectly still, his eyes closed, and filtered out the familiar noises, the gentle lap of the tide, the prayer bell tinkle from the rigging of yachts moored in the outer harbour. When the sound came again he had it so perfectly identified that he indulged in a moment's self-congratulation. The amazing microchip man. Pushing forty-five and running to fat, yet he could still do the trick. One second fast asleep, the next wide awake and ready for action, the coiled spring. Bogan lay still breathing carefully, letting his heart rate settle. He was remembering a friend of his, a fireman, same age, who could do the same instant wake-up whenever the bells went down in the middle of the night. Leap into action. Only once he grabbed the pole and by the time his boots hit the apron in the engine house three floors below he was dead from a massive heart attack. After that, Bogan learned to pace himself.

When his pulse was down to normal, he opened one eye and confirmed his surroundings. He was lying on the pull-down bunk in the main cabin of a 40-foot Master Marine cruiser called *Dancing Lady*, the deckhead swaying slightly as the fibreglass hull rolled gently on the swell. The cabin cruiser was one of a clutch of pleasure craft snuggled up inside the inner harbour, moored to the pontoons of the exclusive Dolphin Marina.

Bogan opened the other eye and took in the plump woman lying beside him. But for carmine nail polish on fingers and toes, a gold choker at her throat, diamond stud earrings and a knuckleduster selection of rings, she was naked, her large breasts rising like a small mountain range as she slept off their earlier exertions, the musk of dried sweat sharpening the boudoir scent of expensive perfume. Bogan made a show of yawning and stretching; then, careful not to wake her, rolled slowly off the crumpled bunk, pulled on his faded blue jeans, pushed his feet into canvas loafers and began a shambling shuffle towards the head. In the narrow passageway which led aft to the cockpit he moved swiftly, reaching in to flush the mechanism, then darting under the canopy and slipping over the side as he tugged his zip, fastened his belt, and pulled a sweatshirt over his head.

He was already running when his feet hit the boardwalk of the pontoon, crouched low, sprinting between the lines of boats for the only access to the marina, a stucco archway which led to the car park ashore. At the archway he stopped and waited, allowing his breathing to return to normal. He ducked out of sight when he saw the kid approaching, a small smile of triumph playing on his lips. Amateurs, he told himself in self-satisfaction, bloody amateurs.

The kid was about twenty with untidy hair and a bad complexion. He was wearing an anorak over a tracksuit and had the camera slung over his shoulder. His air of casual nonchalance was almost convincing as he came swinging down the wooden slats, heading back to the car he had left in the parking area. As he came through the arch, Bogan's arm shot out and grabbed him in a headlock.

'Gottcha!'

'Hey . . . what . . .' The kid's eyes popped.

'You're trespassing,' Bogan said. 'This is private property.'

'Hey, look,' the kid gasped, 'I was just admiring the boats, that's all.'

'Like hell you were.' Bogan tightened his grip and the kid squealed. 'Now there's two ways we can do this,' Bogan said reasonably. 'Either you give me the camera like a nice sensible lad and we'll part as friends, like none of this ever happened, or you can give me some fast line of bullshit and

I'll throw you in the dock there and stamp on your fingers every time you try to get out. Take your pick, it's all the same to me.'

The kids arms flailed weakly and he gasped for air. 'Look, mister, I didn't do anything . . .'

Bogan gave him a squeeze. 'OK . . . OK!' the kid yelped and offered no resistance as Bogan took the camera from him, released his grip and stepped back still barring the kid's way, raised the Nikon and pressed the trigger. The motorwind whirred, confirming the sound which had wakened him. Bogan snapped the camera open and pulled out the film, exposing it to the light. The kid watched with dull eyes as with a long overarm throw he sent camera and film flying in a high arc to hit the water with a splash and disappear from sight.

'There you go,' Bogan said, grinning now. 'No more happy snaps.' He stepped aside and jerked a thumb towards the car park. 'Now you'd better get out of my sight before I change my mind and give you a ducking too. Oh, and you can tell your boss he can tell Charlie he's wasting his money. He can get dirty pictures from the porn shops, but if he's got something to say to me, all he's got to do is pick up the phone.'

Bogan walked back to the boat feeling pleased with himself. The morning sun dappled the water and out beyond the neat lines of the marina, one of the sea-going yachts was under way. He stepped back on board *Dancing Lady*, ducked under the awning and ambled down the passageway to the cabin.

Madelaine was in the galley making coffee, spooning instant and Coffee-mate into a mug. She had on a cream cotton robe with a nautical motif and mules. She looked round as Bogan appeared in the hatchway. 'Well . . . well . . . I open my eyes and wait for my morning kiss and what do I find? My able seaman's gone adrift. Don't tell me you've taken up jogging?'

Bogan grinned. 'Just a constitutional, Maddie. Nothing like a little exercise before breakfast.'

She arched an eyebrow. 'I seem to recall you prefer other ways of keeping fit. You want some coffee?'

'Sure,' Bogan said. 'Make it strong. We had a visitor this morning.'

She froze. 'A what?'

'A visitor. Kid with a camera getting snaps of you and me at play. I thought you said Charlie wasn't the jealous type.'

'What's Charlie got to do with it?'

'Well, who do you think's going to send a peeper snooping around to get the dirt on us? Your old man, that's who.'

Her eyes flashed. 'The little creep. I'll wring his scrawny neck when I get my hands on him. You mean someone was out there taking pictures of us?'

Bogan gulped down the coffee. It tasted good. 'Take it easy,' he said. 'I caught him and told him his fortune. His camera's at the bottom of the dock. I thought you said all Charlie was interested in these days was his TV commercials and his gas barbecue.'

'I'm going to barbecue him, the little shit, he starts giving me a hard time. He's going to find out what hard times are really like.'

'Hey, come on, don't get excited. Nothing I can't handle. I was just curious. I thought Charlie was too busy flogging his double glazing and playing with his toys to care what his missus was up to.' Bogan shrugged. 'I just don't like surprises, that's all. Maybe we ought to give it a rest for a while until we know for sure what he's up to. I don't fancy snoopers following me around.'

Maddie said, 'He's got a nerve. I could've cooked his goose any time I wanted to, only it was never worth the bother. He does his thing and I do mine, and that's the way it's going to stay. He thinks I don't know what he gets up to with those little girls down at the TV studio. Well, he's got another think coming.'

Bogan said, 'Yeah, well, maybe he's getting possessive now he thinks he's a tycoon. All that TV exposure's gone to his head.' He drained his coffee mug and put an arm around her shoulder and gave her a squeeze. 'Don't you worry your pretty head about it. If he wants trouble, he can have trouble.' Bogan's lip twisted into a mirthless smile. 'Next time he takes those bimbos out for a cruise on this thing I'll slip a little cannabis into his footlocker and give Customs a bell. They're hot as mustard on illegal importation. We'll see how the TV star likes that kind of publicity.'

He looked at his watch, pulled her around to face him and gave her a long, reassuring kiss. Her eyes grew misty. 'Come back to bed,' she murmured. 'I'm getting randy again.'

Bogan shook his head. 'One thing you rich ladies never could get through your head: mugs like us got to make a crust. Got to go to work.'

CHAPTER 3

Michael said they were going to be rich. Jojo could picture him saying it, with that big wide smile on his face, coming up the slip in his wetsuit, tanks slung over his shoulder. It was summer and he was having a fine time with the tourists, his thick black hair slicked back, the wetsuit showing off his muscles, the wind and the sun combining to give his face the weatherbeaten complexion of a latterday pirate. Oh, he looked the part all right, and he played the part too, all those salty tales of diving on the wrecks and wrestling with the sharks out in the Sound. There weren't any sharks within a hundred miles, but he didn't let a detail like that spoil the yarns he'd spin for the customers. Acting up for the punters he called it, and they practically drooled over him.

She could see him walking up the concrete slip with that lithe casual swagger of his, ambling up to where she was waiting with the pick-up and telling her they were going to be rich with such absolute sincerity that she believed him. That was their first summer together and she wanted it to last forever, but when the seasons changed, the sea chilled and the trade dropped off he took contracts on the North Sea rigs, going up to Aberdeen for a couple of months at a stretch, risking his hide in the treacherous icy waters servicing the wellheads on the sea bed to keep the crude pumping. But however hard they tried, freelance divers didn't get rich, that was the fallacy. Only accountants and lawyers made real money, but Michael could never see that.

Jojo continued to work at Nightingale's, the estate agents in Vine Street, and carved herself a niche looking after the business of buying up small rundown terraces near the docks and engaging small-time jobbing builders to do them up so that with a facelift and a lick of paint the two-up two-downs could be sold at a handsome profit as bijou harbourside cottages. The weekend sailors eager for the raffish bohemian scene of the waterfront snapped them up.

'You know your trouble, Jojo,' Carol told her over cappuccinos in the coffee shop across the street from the office. 'You've never had it rough. You've never walked around town on a Saturday afternoon with the rain dripping down your neck, looking in the shop windows with nothing in your purse.'

'Neither have you,' Jojo said. 'Since when did you ever have to scrape along?'

'I'm just making the point, that's all,' Carol said. 'Look at you, you've got everything you want, a nice place, a good job and Mr come-to-bed eyes.'

'Oh, so that's it. You and Derek had another row.'

'Don't talk to me about that fat slob. He comes home, flops on the couch in his dirty clothes yelling for his tea. So I cook something nice for him, what's he do? Smothers it with HP sauce and wolfs it down, don't even taste it. I could put dogs' turds on his plate and it'd be the same thing, shovel it in and then flake out on the couch again watching the snooker. I say something to him, I might just as well be talking to the wall for all the good it does me. I want to go to the pictures, what's he say? Snooker on the TV. End of story. If there was a religion required eight hours watching a couple of dummies walking around a table poking coloured balls with sticks, he'd be the bishop or something. So I do the washing and the ironing and whatever until I'm bored out of my skull. As far as he's concerned, I might as well not exist. I bet your Michael pays you more attention than that.'

Jojo smiled. 'Well, he could care less about snooker.'

'Young love.' Carol shook her head. 'That's what I thought. Only take a tip from me, keep him on a tight leash. Not that Derek was ever anything but a slob, only I made the mistake of giving him too much leeway and he got hooked on this snooker thing. Never played himself, of course, he couldn't raise the energy, but to hear him talk you'd think he was the world-ranking expert. Once he's glued to the box his eyes sort of glaze over and he gets that silly smirk on his face and there's no shifting him. You know what I think it is?'

'What d'you think it is?' Jojo asked with an indulgent smile.

Carol looked serious. 'I read an article in a magazine once about how you could send invisible messages through the TV, ones you couldn't see and they hypnotized anyone who was watching.'

'Subliminal,' Jojo said.

'Yeah, that was the word. What I think is, they're sending Derek messages like that with all this snooker rubbish and they've burned out all the circuits in his brain. There can't be any other reason he could sit there mesmerized for so long.'

'What happens when there's no snooker on?'

'That's even worse. Switch off the TV and it's like you turned off his life-support system. He staggers up to bed and then he gets this idea he's going to make love to me. You know Derek's idea of good sex? He don't bother with any warm-up, just heaves himself on top of me like a sack of potatoes and all the sweet talking I ever get is a lot of grunting and gasping and then it's all over. I think thirty seconds was his all-time record.'

'My, but you're bitter today,' Jojo said.

'I just think to myself there's got to be more to life than being a snooker widow who's sleeping with a pig.' Carol drank some coffee and collected froth on her upper lip. She gazed longingly across at the glass-fronted counter where the pastries were on display. 'To hell with the diet, I'm famished. I'm going to have an apple and custard Danish, can I get you one?'

Jojo shook her head. She watched her friend's ample figure squeezed into a mini-dress wobble over to the counter and then return with the cakes. She began to laugh, suddenly imagining Carol and Derek heaving and grunting like a couple of porkers. Carol's face hardened. 'You think that's funny? You wait. Right now you've got it made, but your turn'll come, Miss Stars-in-your eyes, believe me. Whatever they look like on the outside, underneath men are just all sorts of selfish bastards. It just takes a while to discover which variety you've got.'

Quite why she recalled that snippet of conversation at that instant Jojo couldn't imagine. She sat cocooned in the opulent cockpit of the Jaguar and stared at the sleek lines of the Arrow Bridge. Traffic was moving on the span, building up to the rush hour. The bridge was stretching and yawning and coming alive. Just what kind of a bastard Michael would turn out to be, she would not discover until much later. And now that she knew it didn't much matter. She sat in the driver's seat of the Jaguar with her hands resting on the steering-wheel and stared at the bridge. She began to wonder how far Michael had travelled by now and whether, if she screwed up her courage, she could still catch him up.

CHAPTER 4

Bogan drove to work in the silver Astra GTE he had on permanent loan from a used car dealer for whom he did favours. He turned into the police station yard and parked carelessly in the slot marked 'Emergency Vehicles Only'. He got out of the car and walked down the wire mesh tunnel they used to transfer prisoners and let himself in through the blank reinforced door with his card key.

He was on his way up to the single men's quarters on the top floor when he saw the door to the burglary squad was open and the office was empty. Probably all swilling coffee in the canteen, Bogan thought, typical CID, coppers indoors he called them with a sneer, for he had little time for the detectives who looked like bank clerks these days and spent most of their time pushing paper around. He went inside, picked up the phone on the nearest desk, dialled a number and told the snooty bitch who answered the call with a sing-song 'Good morning, Murray and Company, how may I help you?' to put him through to Iris in accounts. He stood there, his irritation growing as a doorbell version of 'Greensleeves' played in his ear. The tinny music which was supposed to soothe callers as they waited for their connection cut off abruptly.

'I told you not to call me at the office.' Just hearing her voice still made him tingle.

Bogan said, 'How're you doing?'

'I was all right until this phone rang. How many times have I got to tell you don't call me here. I'm not supposed to take private calls in the firm's time, they've got a rule.'

'I just wanted to know how you are, that's all. That a crime all of a sudden? Tell 'em I'm a customer.'

'You come on the phone, you practically bit Jean's head

off, you think they don't know who you are? Any minute now I'm going to have the supervisor coming over here giving me a hard time and that's something I can do without, thank you very much. Get off the line, Bogan.'

'Hey, come on, say something nice to me.'

'Oh, for God's sake.'

'Look, what about the weekend, we could take a drive out, have a drink at a country pub, a few laughs. You used to like that.'

'You never give up, do you? Let me tell you for the hundredth time. I don't want to see you, I don't want to talk to you, I don't want to know you. Now you stop pestering me or I'm going to call my solicitor and get him to do something you're not going to like one little bit. You got that through your thick skull?'

'You sound terrific when you're mad, you know that? Turns me to jelly. All I was thinking is we could have dinner, a bottle of wine, where's the harm?'

'You're sick, Bogan. I'm hanging up.'

'Wait! Just think about it, Iris, where's the harm—'

The line was dead. Not even 'Greensleeves', just silence.

'I'll call again,' Bogan muttered to himself. 'Maybe she'll change her mind.'

He put the phone down and turned around. One of the new breed detectives, a smoothie of a DC with a taste for designer clothes named Dave Harris, was leaning against the doorjamb watching him with an amused expression. 'Sounds like you got the brush-off, Bogan. You want to try grab-a-granny night down at the Tinsel Town, you could strike lucky.'

'Why don't you get stuffed, Dave?' Bogan said flatly. He wasn't in the mood.

'I heard about you telephone perverts,' Harris said, his smile widening into a grin. 'Ringing up housewives and asking them what colour knickers they're wearing.'

'Do me a favour,' Bogan said. 'Drop dead.'

'My, my, aren't we touchy. I bet you didn't get your shredded wheat this morning.'

The baiting brought a tight expression to Bogan's face. 'You feel somebody blowing in your ear last night, Dave?'

The detective shrugged the shoulders of his Valentino jacket, still grinning.

Bogan said, ''Cause I was having a quiet drink with Harry Welsh and your name came up.'

'Oh yeah?' The grin began to fade.

Bogan walked towards the door. 'Me and old Harry go way back, joined the job together, long, long ago.'

The grin disappeared. Welsh was the Detective-Superintendent who had the power of God over the CID. A flick of an eyebrow could send a promising young DC back into uniform.

'What d'you mean, my name came up?'

'We were just talking, that's all.' Bogan's face turned wolfish. 'Sure you didn't feel a hot tongue in your ear?'

Harris scowled. 'OK, what'd he say about me?'

Bogan flexed his shoulders. 'He said you were a wanker, and I agreed.'

He walked out of the office and went up to the single men's where he had a shoebox which contained a bed and a locker. The stale air was musty from unwashed clothes strewn around. A half-eaten Chinese takeaway had congealed in a tinfoil container perched on the sill of the only window which looked out on to the blank wall of an air shaft. The cheap brown carpet was stained and dirty and an amber glass ashtray purloined from the clubroom overflowed with cigarette butts. Even Bogan, who was normally impervious to the male odours of his cave, wrinkled his nose in disgust at his own squalor, slipped his feet out of the trainers, dropped his jeans and kicked them into a corner. He pulled the sweatshirt over his head, cast it on the floor and stood for a moment, yawning and stretching, his hirsute belly overhanging the elastic of his boxer shorts, in sharp contrast to the alabaster white spindles of his legs rasped hairless by years of friction from the rough serge of police issue trousers. Still yawning, Bogan opened the locker, took out an electric razor, blew on the shaver head, sending up a cloud of dust, and ran the buzzing machine over the heavy shadow which blurred his jaw.

He was thinking about the cocky detective downstairs who'd tried taking the mickey. Well, he'd planted a seed of doubt in his mind all right, given him something bitter to chew on for the rest of the day. Then he thought about Iris with the usual twinge of regret and consoled himself with the memory of Charlie Choake's chubby wife and the sensation of burying his face in her pliant breasts and nibbling on nipples like small purple plums. How he'd caught that little rat of a peeper and put him out of business. Oh yes, he cheered himself, nobody put one over on Ted Bogan and got away with it, he was too fly for that. And now he had another brand new day ahead of him, doing what he was good at, wheeling and dealing and manipulating people to his own ends, the culmination of all those years on the street. Even the mean room in which he spent as little time as possible was a perfect tribute to his go to hell philosophy.

Bogan peered at the reflection of his face in the square of mirror taped inside the locker door and ran the razor carefully over the creases and crevices which gave his face a battered and forlorn look. 'Iris, Iris, look what you've done to me,' he muttered and as he shaved, peering at his own dismal image, something strange happened. The face in the glass changed, became smoother, younger, boyish even. Instead of pouchy and heavy-lidded, the eyes grew brighter, more hopeful. For a fanciful moment Bogan allowed the illusion to linger, transporting him back into his memory, back to the way things had been when he and Iris were together. He could see her now, raven-haired and willowy, his green-eyed fiery nemesis. Ted and Iris. In another time they would have been described as a handsome couple, yet in fifteen years their fragile marriage had yawed from the joy of enslaved lovers to the bitterness of defeated expectations.

Their lives had crossed by chance at the mausoleum of the Crown Court where Bogan, on attachment to the crime squad as a plainclothes aide, had been saddled with the drudgery of exhibits officer in a six-week trial which revolved around a payroll robbery. Iris, an accounts clerk at the transport firm where the robbery took place, was summoned as a prosecution witness, required to attend every day although she was never called to the box. Kicking their heels in the gloomy corridors of the musty court building, they were thrown together for the alchemy of physical attraction to play its mischievous joke.

Bewitched, Bogan set out to woo her by hamming up the part of the swashbuckling detective, recounting tales of daring crime-fighting over endless cups of watery coffee in the draughty canteen. So obsessively did he pursue her that Iris was swept off her feet, oblivious of the true, brutalizing nature of his work. And Bogan, who had always considered himself something of a ladies' man, found himself besotted with her and after a whirlwind courtship they were married.

But based on the quicksand of fancy, their union was always a frail vessel adrift on a sea of storms, and Bogan, back in uniform, soon tired of the pretence and little by little Iris discovered that the heady romance of a cop's life was just an illusion.

As always when he reached this painful point of memory Bogan saw himself back in the ranch-style split-level, one of a select clutch of desirable homes on the heights overlooking the gorge with BMWs and Golf GTIs on the sculptured drives. Even with his rent allowance and Iris working, the mortgage was crippling after the flat in a far less salubrious quarter where they had first set up home. The expression in those days was upwardly mobile and somehow Iris managed the money, made the payments which bled them white and took an inordinate pride in the swanky address which gave them the entree to a new social set. But the corrosion of disenchantment was already leaking into their relationship as Iris learned another painful lesson: a cop's wife makes few friends outside the incestuous orbit of the police world.

Bitterness was setting in and in company she forbade him to mention his work, shooting warning glances whenever the subject came up, brushing aside the casual inquiries by describing him as a 'security consultant'. To please her, Bogan played along with the charade for a while, even to the point of leaving his uniform at the station and changing in the locker-room at the start and end of each shift. But it wasn't enough. With the hurt of betrayal in those green eyes, Iris began to cajole him into doing something more worthwhile with his life than wallowing in the sewers of the city. She scoured the papers and pushed job adverts across the breakfast bar, and still Bogan humoured her until the night she invited Ralph and Denise to supper and Ralph, a self-satisfied pillar of the Rotary Club who ran his own export business, leaned across the debris of the meal to light his cigar from the candle flame and casually offered Bogan a job as his security man. The women exchanged glances and it was so obviously a set-up that Bogan choked on his own bile, cornered, forced to chose between the monastic camaraderie of the force and a wife who despised his work. When he bluntly turned the offer down, Iris didn't speak to him for a week. After that he began to stay on after work for a few drinks, volunteered for overtime and prisoner escorts which took him out of town. Bogan had made his choice, refused to sever the umbilical, and from that moment on his marriage was on a downhill slide until the day Iris could take no more and threw him out.

Rocking forward, Bogan peered more closely into his reflection and broke the spell. Once more that cynical world weary face stared back at him, concealing the emotional scars which left him the way he was now, oh, still the ladies' man, but this time around hunting his women with the cold instincts of a predator, just conquests to be exploited, chalked up and cast aside. But however hard he steeled himself, at introspective moments like this his heart still bled for Iris.

Bogan switched off the razor, replaced it on the cluttered shelf and reached into the rack for his uniform. He kept it in a nylon suit hanger, the trousers and tunic carefully pressed, a fresh white shirt newly laundered. The uniform was a fetish with him. It had to be perfect.

Bogan spread the light blue bag on the cot, ran the zip down and took out the shirt, inspected it for the slightest blemish and, satisfied, put it on. He stepped into the trousers, careful not to disturb the knife-edge crease, zipped the fly and fastened the buckle of the leather belt, clipped on his handcuff pouch and slid his truncheon into the long, concealed pocket inside the leg, leaving the leather strap hanging outside in the quick draw position.

Returning to the mirror, Bogan tied a double Windsor in the black Terylene tie he always wore, scorning the knitted clip-on which was standard issue because it was designed to be strangle-proof, and put on the half-belt tunic with the silver collar dogs and his number, 482, in chrome numerals on the epaulettes. Perched on the edge of the cot, he pulled on black cotton socks and, leaning forward, reached into the bottom of the locker for his Docs which were polished to a high gloss. Bogan examined the shine, gave them a final buff with a tissue, sprinkled Dr Scholl's into each one and then slid his feet into the soft leather boots with a sensation of primitive pleasure. Some of the smart-ass rookies these days went out on the street in cheap plastic shoes or even slip-ons, but Bogan had long ago learned the wisdom of caring for his feet, the trick of walking an eight-hour beat whatever the weather without the misery of blisters and corns. Carefully broken-in Docs had carried him over more miles of pavement than he cared to remember and so he tended them with care and affection, pulling the laces snug against his ankles and tying them off. He stood up, rocking on his heels, reached into the locker for a roll of Sellotape from which he tore a strip, reversed it across the fingers of his right hand and patted himself down with the sticky tape to remove any traces of lint from his uniform.

Bogan turned to the locker for the last time, reached up to the top shelf and took down a clear plastic bag which contained his helmet. He took it out and inspected it. The enamel badge which he refused to surrender for the plastic replicas which were the order of the day gleamed back at him. The nap was brushed to a dull sheen and the ornaments, the twin rosettes and the chrome ventilator, were burnished until they sparkled.

The transformation was complete. Within the space of a few minutes amid the squalor of his cubbyhole Bogan had emerged a butterfly from the chrysalis. Now he stood there, the spit-shined immaculate policeman, looking for all the world as if he had just stepped out of a recruiting poster.

But to the discerning eye there was one almost insignificant feature on the uniform of the immaculate policeman which cast light upon the character of Ted Bogan. Above the left breast pocket of his tunic there was stitched a narrow blue and white campaign ribbon. To a fellow initiate of the brotherhood the ribbon told the story of how the man who wore it had been accepted into the closed community and had passed through the labyrinthine levels of the monastic order, completing each ritual, succeeding in each arcane test of will until he was accorded the highest accolade. The immaculate policeman had stepped up smartly and had raised a snow-white glove in a drill manual salute to receive the Long Service and Good Conduct Medal from the Chief Constable. Twenty-two unblemished years in the force earned him the right to wear the ribbon on his tunic, the ribbon which said that behind this strip of tape stands a capo of the canteen mafia.

Without a backward glance, Bogan left the shambles of his room and went down into the working area of the station. The building was old and dilapidated, the walls of the corridors had over the years absorbed many coats of institutional grey until they were now blotched and mottled. The composition floor had been slicked into a shiny black marble by the tramp of countless feet, and the thick stale air stirred only by the updraughts from the creaking central heating radiators carried the fetid odours of a building exhausted from the grind of twenty-four-hour habitation without respite.

Bogan walked into the parade room and looked around. He saw a row of battered cabinets and a mismatched assortment of metal tables pushed together to form an island in the centre. The room was deserted, but had the look of having been recently vacated. On one wall a notice-board was festooned with thumbtacked photocopies of the latest divisional orders, memos and instructions which blew into the station's admin system like a blizzard. Codfish eyes of suspects stared at him from an artless montage of mug shots. Beside a row of name-tagged skippets there was a wooden rack which held the personal radios hooked up to a charger which kept the batteries topped up. Bogan took one from the rack, hung the set from his belt, threaded the wire under his tunic and clipped the microphone to his lapel under his chin. He sensed a presence behind him, turned around and saw that Davies was standing in the doorway with fists resting on his hips. He had slicked-back hair and a moustache trimmed so close that it looked like the merest shadow on his upper lip.

'The hell time you call this, Bogan?'

'Show time,' Bogan said, unperturbed by the anger flashing in the other man's eyes.

'You missed the briefing.'

Bogan shrugged. 'So I missed the briefing.'

'So I missed the briefing what.'

'So I missed the briefing, Sergeant.' He smiled to show that he didn't mind playing their little games.

'That's more like it,' Davies said. He was the new sergeant on the shift, the chevrons still sitting uncomfortably on his arms, and so he considered himself the front line supervisor. 'Don't push your luck with me, Bogan. I don't know how it was before I came on the scene, and to be frank I don't care. You're on my shift now and you don't come sauntering in here any time you please, you attend the briefings. Got that?'

'Got it, Sarge.'

'You could've missed something important.'

'I don't think so,' Bogan said. 'I could recite the briefing to you from memory. It's just the same bullshit every time. Give 'em the pep talk, assign the beats, send everybody out rejoicing and eager to serve and protect the good people of this fine city, who, if the truth were known, couldn't give a toss as long as they personally don't get raped, mugged, burgled or molested in the park. Then they scream blue murder.'

'For Christ's sake, Bogan.' Davies changed tack. 'The time you've got in, OK, so you've seen it all before and it's all a big yawn, only you're supposed to set an example to the new guys.'

'You want me to do my John Wayne impression, Sarge?'

'You know what I mean. Look at the roster, I've got two off sick, three suspended on that Burton thing, so I'm left parading six PCs and four of them are pro cons still wet behind the ears. You and Taylor are the only two experienced men I've got holding this shift together. We get through the day, we're going to be lucky. You don't turn up for the briefing, and Taylor looks like death warmed up, what're the others going to think?'

Bogan looked down at the sergeant's shoes. Davies's hobby was ballroom dancing and he had nimble little feet. The shoes were patent leather slip-ons.

'The meter's running, Sarge. You want to tango or you want me out on the street? It's all the same to me.'

Davies's face flushed and his expression hardened. 'You're a chancer, Bogan, you know that? Well, I've got news'll wipe that smirk off your face. You're the nursemaid. You're pushing the pram today.'

'What?'

'You heard me. You're the tutor this shift. You've got Wilcox with you.'

'Oh, come on, Sarge,' Bogan protested, smarting from the sucker punch. 'That's not fair. I don't do kindergarten stuff. I always work by myself.'

'You'd've turned up for the briefing I might have thought twice. Now you take what's dished up. You're showing Wilcox the ropes, no argument.'

'Oh, for Christ's sake.'

'Oh, for Christ's sake nothing.' Davies jutted his chin in triumph. 'Think yourself lucky you've still got the Incident Car, and don't go teaching the kid any bad habits. He's a graduate, remember, lots of brainpower, going to be chief one day, so you take good care of him.'

'Honest to God, I don't know what the job's coming to.' Bogan was mortified. 'All of a sudden we're falling all over ourselves to take on dreamy kids just because they've got a degree in plasticine modelling. Everybody knows they're worse then useless on the street, so what happens? Minute you turn your back, they're all inspectors tucked up in nice warm offices. Makes you sick.'

'Bogan, you're prehistoric.' Davies prodded the raw nerve he'd just uncovered. 'You're looking at the future. Brain, not brawn.'

'Oh yeah,' Bogan said. 'Well, I was on the miners' strike. Went up there with the PSUs. I was on the bloody picket line when all hell broke loose. I got whacked over the head with a placard said LESBIAN STUDENTS SUPPORT THE NUM. I had my brains beat out by some brawny dyke from some poxy university.'

Davies rubbed it in, 'You don't like it, you can always put your ticket in.'

Bogan sneered. 'And hand the job over to a bunch of pansies who're a disgrace to the uniform?'

'Then you're going to have to lump it,' Davies said, ''cause, like it or not, you've got our very own Brain of Britain under your wing for the rest of the day, so do me a favour, shove your prejudices. You never know, the kid might teach you a thing or two.'

'Yeah, well, I'm taking this up with my Federation rep,' Bogan said.

'Do what you like on your own time, Bogan,' Davies said, 'but right now you're bellyaching on mine, so let's get the lead out.'

Experience had taught Bogan a million ways to get his own back on this bantam cock of a sergeant, but now was neither the time nor the place. He gritted his teeth and was on his way out of the parade room when Davies performed a nimble *chassée*, cut him off and socked him again. 'Oh, and just so we understand each other, don't even think about pulling the wool with me. I've got your number. I've heard all about this "cheaper than Securicor" caper, so don't let me catch you skiving off on the fiddle, or I'll come down on you like a ton of bricks.'

Bogan feigned an injured look. 'Who, me, Sergeant?' he protested innocently.

Beyond the working area of the station stretched the executive wing, a corridor hung with sepia prints of old-time law men in collared tunics glowering from behind handlebar moustaches. Past the typing pool, already ringing to the mahjong clatter of word-processors, and the admin office awash with computer printouts conveying the latest batch of instructions from headquarters, stood an oak-panelled door on which a brass nameplate proclaimed Sub-Divisional Commander. On the far side of the door Superintendent Bert Royal was tinkering with his new toy, a filter coffee machine which he had set up on the top of a low bookcase to one side of his desk. He was a thickset man in his late fifties, almost completely bald, with expressive brown eyes which could switch from mirth to displeasure in the space of a blink. He was wearing a uniform shirt from which the epaulettes of his rank were missing, the cuffs rolled up on his forearms as his stubby fingers moulded a paper cone. He scooped coffee into the filter, wrinkling his nose in pleasure at the aroma.

'Colombian,' Royal announced without turning around. 'Got to have it ground just right, that's the trick, not too fine or it goes to dust and you lose the flavour.'

Now he turned, smiling, a cherub pleased with himself. 'The stuff they used to bring me from out there—' he waved a hand towards the typing pool which ministered to his needs—'ugh, tasted like dishwater. I mean, I'm only the gaffer around here, so I said, "What do I have to do to get a decent cup of coffee?" Mavis and the girls went out and got me this little beauty. They said it was worth it so I wouldn't be like a bear with a sore head all day. Me, can you imagine that?'

The girl with the wavy chestnut hair sitting in the easy chair on the far side of the desk gave him a broad grin.

'Never let it be said, Uncle Bert.'

Royal looked at her as the coffee brewed. The neat grey two-piece with the shadow stripe, the blue silk blouse, the skirt riding just above the knee showing off the curve of her crossed legs, sheer stockings, a midnight blue suede court shoe with a silver buckle dancing on her raised foot. His smile grew wistful. 'Been a long time since I bounced you on my knee, young lady.'

The machine groaned and gurgled and he turned back and watched the level rise in the jug. When the process was complete he poured two cups and handed one to his visitor. 'Rank hath its privilege,' he said. 'Decent coffee. Try it like it is, no milk or sugar, oh, unless—' he reached down to the bottom drawer of his desk and brought out an unlabelled bottle of clear liquid—'you want to try a drop of this with it to keep the chill out, Plum brandy, gift from some visiting firemen from Romania, got a kick like rocket fuel.' He poured a slug into both cups and then came around the desk to sink into the other easy chair. He appraised the girl again and shook his head in wonder. 'Whatever happened to that little tomboy used to terrorize those CID parties?' He spread his hands. 'Inspector Vicky Rivers, all grown up. Your old man could see you now, God rest his soul, he'd sure as hell be proud of you.'

Vicky sipped her coffee, watching him over the rim of the cup. 'Phooey, you know he never wanted me in the job, tried to put me off all the time.'

'Fathers and daughters,' Royal said. 'You were his little girl. They treated women like dirt in the force in those days, he just didn't want you to get hurt.'

'Well he did his damnedest. After I applied, I don't think he spoke to me for a month.'

'You inherited his stubborn streak,' Royal chuckled. 'Underneath that cast-iron exterior he was as soft as marshmallow. I ought to know, I was his oppo back in the good old days.' He wagged his head, remembering. 'Jack Rivers, the best CID chief this force ever had.'

'He used to carry his case files around in a Sainsbury's bag,' Vicky recalled. 'Never survive now, not with PACE and HOLMES and all the smart stuff.'

'Yeah, you're right,' Royal agreed. 'I remember when

they tried to put a terminal in his office.' He glanced across at the COMCON computer sitting on its table on the far side of his desk, just part of the furniture. 'Old Jack blew his top, tapped his temple and told the whizzkids he'd already got all the computer he needed up there. They left it, but he never touched it. He was the last of the old school, worked on instinct; sweat a suspect a couple of days just on a hunch.'

'Not any more,' Vicky said. 'Those days are long gone.'

'More's the pity,' Royal complained with feeling. 'All this please and thank-you before you lock anybody up. The way we mollycoddle suspects these days, Jack must be spinning in his grave. He only lost one case, you know that, Vicky, in all those years.'

'The moneylender. What was his name?'

'Benjamin Isaacs,' Royal recalled as he pushed up from the chair and went over to the bookcase. 'Little shylock battered to death in his shop down by the docks.' He slid open the glass door, rummaged between the books and brought out a two-foot-long iron bar, rusty and pitted. 'The one that got away.' He turned with the bar resting across the palms of his hands like an offering. 'This was the murder weapon. Old Jack had it mounted on a wooden stand and kept it on his desk. You'd go in there at night and see him with a glass of Scotch in his hand just staring at it, like he was trying to will it to talk to him.'

Royal hefted the bar in his meaty hand. 'That one gnawed away at him. He couldn't accept that some toe-rag with the luck of the devil could outsmart him. When they were clearing out the office after he pegged it, I picked it up as a souvenir. Stubborn as a mule, your old man.'

Vicky said, 'You know, all I ever wanted was to follow in his footsteps, but he used to get that supercilious curl on his lip and tell me crime investigation was man's work. In his book careers for women were strictly limited to hairdressing and frock shops, or better still, chained to the kitchen sink.'

'He would have been proud of you, all the same.' Royal repeated the compliment, leaning back against the edge of his desk, drinking his coffee and admiring her. 'His little girl an inspector at what, twenty-six?'

'Twenty-seven,' Vicky said. 'And attitudes haven't changed much. When I got through my last board I told 'em I wanted CID and you could see they didn't take me seriously. Oh, they'll let us girls do DC and DS, but DI? Could mean giving crusty old detectives orders, now wouldn't that be heresy, even from Jack Rivers's daughter. Why not try schools liaison, community involvement?'

Royal smiled. He could picture the scene. 'You're too pretty, Vicky, that's your problem. All the women DIs I ever knew had moustaches and were built like brick outhouses. You don't fit the profile.'

'So when this job came up, I put in for it,' Vicky said, 'and you know the only reason I got it, Uncle Bert? Nobody else applied.'

'Oh, I can believe that,' Royal said with feeling. 'You go in the canteen now, you're going to see everyone else disappearing out of the door. Won't make you any friends.'

'It's what I joined to do, investigation,' Vicky said, her face suddenly serious. 'If I can't get in through the front door, I'll sneak in through the back.'

She said it with such conviction that Bert Royal was reminded of his old partner. When Jack Rivers set his mind on something, nothing stopped him. Pig-headed, stubborn, like a terrier worrying a bone. All the same, he wondered how this slip of a girl was going to cope, swimming with the sharks at headquarters. He pulled the lobe of an ear in thought. Then he asked, 'So how're they treating you up at the dream factory?'

She gave him a knowing look. 'Oh, I'm still a novelty. They keep opening doors for me, all smiles, watching their language, just waiting for me to fall flat on my face.'

'Well, you're flying close to the sun there, Vicky, on the Dep's team, and you know what he's like, loves to play it close to the chest. One day they're going to open that safe of his and Shergar and Lord Lucan'll jump out.'

Vicky laughed as she reached for the slim Samsonite briefcase parked beside her chair. 'On that note, do you think we could get down to business?'

The pleasure faded slowly from Royal's face as he came back to the reason for Inspector Vicky Rivers's visit to his office. The thought did not fill him with joy. Frowning, he sorted among the clutter on his desktop and found the epaulettes which bore the crown of his rank and fitted them to the loops on his shirt. He rolled the sleeves down and fastened the cuffs, assumed the gravity of command. He went around the desk and dropped solidly into the swivel chair. Then with a sigh which was almost audible he leaned forward and rested his forearms on the blotter. 'I hope you're not going to give me a hard time, Inspector.' He meant it as a joke, but Vicky hauled the briefcase on to her lap, thumbed the catches and took out a thick buff file which she set on the desk between them. She looked into Royal's face with a level, unblinking gaze.

'Not unless you force me to, sir,' she said with such severity that Bert Royal winced, taken aback. Behind that pretty face there was vintage Jack Rivers giving him the ball-bearing stare.

CHAPTER 5

A black Orion turned off the North Shore Drive and came down the approach road to the Arrow Bridge, slowed as it passed the lay-by, stopped and reversed, coming to a halt on the double yellows opposite the parking area. A Garfield grinned from the rear window. In the front of the Ford two young men in sports shirts and sunglasses craned their necks for a better view of the cluster of cars in the pull-in.

'Bingo!' the driver said.

'The banana split,' the passenger said.

'The very same.' The driver beat a tattoo on the steering-wheel with his fingers. 'We just hit the jackpot.'

'After that shambles this morning I could use some luck,' the passenger said, reaching into the glove box and taking out a sheaf of papers. He ran his thumb down a list of registration numbers, pointed one out to the driver and laughed. 'A dead racing cert, Paul. Silly sod didn't even change the plates.'

Paul said, 'What'd I tell you, Russ? We look long enough and hard enough, we'd find it sooner or later.'

'Tell you the truth,' Russ said, 'I had my choice I'd rather I'd got lucky earlier in the day, before Ron tore me off a strip. Practically chewed my head off. I mean, I'm up all night freezing half to death getting pictures of the bloke at it with his bit of stuff on the boat. So I go in for the close-up and the guy clocks me, big bastard nearly throttled me, and he threw my camera in the dock.'

'You mean Ron's camera. Yeah, I can see how Ron might've been a trifle disappointed in that. His camera goes in the drink and he's out of pocket a hundred quid or so, and he's got to tell the client he didn't get the pictures of his naughty wife he promised him.' Paul shook his head.

'How many times have I got to tell you you don't do the David Bailey routine on a tricky obbo like that. You lie way back and use the long Tom. I remember I did one on a caravan once, hid in the woods for two days and waited 'em out. In the end the thing was rocking so hard I couldn't keep it in focus.'

'If Ron'd told me the mark was a copper who fancied himself as an all-in wrestler, I would've kept my distance. Only he didn't bother with that little detail.'

'You've worked for Ron as long as I have, you learn to read between the lines. He only tells you what he wants to tell you, the rest he keeps up his sleeve. He was on the force thirty years himself before he set up in this game, could even have served with the guy, so he probably feels embarrassed he's got to do a number on him.'

Russ said, 'Well, he didn't feel embarrassed about tearing a strip off me. I thought he was going to have a coronary, he got so mad.'

Paul shrugged. 'Don't take any notice. It's the luck of the draw, you win some, you lose some. Ron knows that. We take in the banana split and we're going to score maximum brownie points.'

They studied the cars in the lay-by, checking out the scene. Then Russ said, 'Yeah, I suppose you're right, only I had my choice I'd rather have got lucky with lover-boy. These snatchbacks . . . I really hate doing these snatchbacks. You sneak up and grab a guy's wheels while his back's turned. It's like . . . it's like cutting his nuts off.'

Paul said, 'Look, in this line of work you've basically got two options. You either go with your principles and starve, or you grab it while you can and eat. Me, I'm old-fashioned. I prefer to eat.'

'Yeah, well,' Russ said, 'it goes against the grain, that's all. A guy's car, it's like part of him. I know what I'd feel like if I had my car snatched.'

'If it makes you feel better,' Paul said, 'it isn't his car. It belongs to the finance company. This big shot made one payment on the hire purchase and they didn't hear from him again. Now they've run out of patience and they want it back. On that thing, his one payment probably wouldn't cover an oil change.'

'I still don't get it,' Russ said. 'I thought this guy was supposed to be smart. I thought you said he'd most likely got that baby squirrelled away in a lock-up somewhere. Tucked up out of sight. Now there it is, out in the open where you can't miss it. You think this could be a set-up? The way my luck's running, he's hiding in there with a twelve-bore or a baseball bat, just waiting for some cool joker to sneak up and then he lets him have it.'

'Nah, you're just letting your imagination run away with you. Nobody can look over both shoulders all the time, he probably just got careless. Now he's going to get car-less.'

'Very funny. I don't care what you say, I've still got a bad feeling on this. The man's too fly to be that stupid.'

'We don't get paid on what we think,' Paul said, 'we get paid on results. Now, unless you've got some cast-iron objection I can see some sense in, we're going to tiptoe over there like the true professionals we're supposed to be and we're going to repossess that motor-car under the powers invested in us by Century Finance. Take about twenty seconds max and we're out of here.'

Russ said, 'Yeah, I suppose you're right. I just hate snatchbacks, that's all. You didn't catch Philip Marlowe or Jim Rockford doing snatchbacks.'

Paul twisted around, leaned into the back seat and retrieved a briefcase. He opened the case on his lap and sorted through a selection of ignition keys, each tagged with the registration number of the vehicle to which they belonged. He found the one he wanted, took it out and closed the case. He held out the key. 'They didn't work for Ron Rowland Investigations either. Now, I'm going to drive fifty yards down the road, do a U-turn and come back up on that side. If it all still looks kosher, you're going to jump out, walk over to that motor, get in the driver's seat, start her up and follow me. We'll get some breakfast on the way back to the office. I'm starving.'

'Why me?' Russ protested.

Paul looked at him, his eyes hidden behind the sunglasses. 'Because you're the dude who's got to impress Ron, otherwise you're out on your ear. I'm the one who spotted it, you're the one brings it in. That's what partners are for, to share the honours.'

The Orion cruised down the road, made a U-turn and headed back towards the parking area. The two men inside watched for anything which would arouse their suspicions. They saw nothing out of the ordinary.

As they drew level with the line of parked cars Russ released his seat-belt and reached into the back seat for his anorak.

'Get it out of there fast,' Paul told him. 'Stick behind me. We'll go to Big Mac and I'll sink my teeth into a quarter-pounder.'

Russ said, 'What if he's in there, having a kip or something?'

'Walk past,' Paul said, 'I'll pick you up down the end there, and we'll sit on him, see what he gets up to. Christ, I'm hungry.'

'What if it's a set-up and he has a go at me?'

'What is this, Twenty Questions?'

'I'm just thinking out loud, that's all. I told you, I hate snatchbacks.'

'Look, you want to be nice to people, go and be a social worker. If he's daft enough to have a pop at you, thump him and run like hell. I'll be just down the end there.'

'Yeah, but what if—'

'For Christ's sake, give it a rest, Russ. Just get on with it, and we can get out of here. My stomach thinks my throat's been cut.'

Russ got out of the Orion, put on his anorak and walked towards the yellow XJS convertible. Yellow with a white hood, the elusive banana split. He was still smarting from his earlier escapade at the marina and his neck hurt when he swallowed. The episode had unnerved him, and so he approached the Jaguar with growing trepidation. It just seemed too good to be true. They'd wasted days on end hunting all over town trying to get a lead on the banana split and suddenly the Jag popped up right under their noses. If ever anything looked like a set-up, this was the one. The car just sitting there, waiting to be found, was unreal. It was all right for Paul, nice and safe in the Orion, foot on the pedal, ready to take off, Russ reflected miserably. He wasn't the one who was going to get a good hiding if it hit the fan.

He approached the Jaguar cautiously from the rear, trying to see inside through the dinky back window in the hood. He couldn't see anything, which only made him more nervous. He moved gingerly along the flank of the car on the driver's side, expecting the door to fly open any second and a fist or other hard instrument to smash him in the face. His mouth went dry and he wished for the hundredth time that morning that he'd told Ron where to stick his lousy job. Now he was abreast of the driver's door, screwing up his nerve to look inside. He gave the car a fast visual once-over and his heart skipped as he realized that it was empty. Relief washed over him and he turned and gave the Orion a thumbs up. Paul waved back, gesturing to make it snappy. Screw you, Russ muttered to himself. He tried a little pressure on the door. It was unlocked and swung open under his hand. The XJS was definitely empty, he could see that now, no one crouched in the narrow space behind the seats. It was going to be cinch after all. Then the perverse notion struck him. If it really was a set-up, the guy would hardly put himself at a disadvantage by sitting in the car. He'd lie in ambush, somewhere handy. Wouldn't he?

The hairs prickled on Russ's neck. He spun around, still holding the car door and every shadow held a new terror. In a panic he threw himself into the driver's seat, crouching down to present a minimum target for the shotgun blast he fully expected. In his anxiety he fumbled the key the first time, then managed to fit it into the ignition and start the engine. The big cat purred.

Russ slammed the T-bar into reverse and gunned out of the parking space, smoking the tyres, punched the lever into drive with the heel of his hand, spun the power steering and took off with an angry growl from the four litres under the bonnet, almost shunting the Orion up ahead which could not match such spectacular acceleration. As he stamped the brake something skittered from under the seat and brushed his foot. Russ eased off and fell in behind the Ford, breathing deeply to let the tension out, calming himself. He'd made it, snatched back the banana split, no sweat. He began to laugh. He was going to walk in on Ron, toss the keys on his desk and demand a bonus. Yeah, a big fat bonus. Something was jammed against his foot. Russ took his eyes off the road for a second and glanced down the footwell. He caught sight of the big ugly knife with the serrated blade and thought at first that the smears were rust. He looked up, blinked and glanced down again. It wasn't rust on the blade. It was blood.

Looking across the desk into those feline eyes, recognizing the cool professional technique of a natural investigator, Bert Royal felt slighted and not a little hurt. All that 'Uncle Bert' stuff! Vicky Rivers was using the wiles she had picked up from the old master to wind him around her finger. All of a sudden, in his own office, safe inside the walls of his own police station, Royal felt discomforted and out of sorts. When Vicky had called from the Lubianka to set up the meeting his natural reluctance to cooperate with the Deputy's rubber heels had been subverted by curiosity. How had Jack Rivers's little girl turned out? Over the years he'd lost track of her career and his difficulty picturing her in a job which was loathed and feared in equal proportions had caused him to drop his guard.

Nobody in their right mind volunteered for the Dep's personal investigation squad, the Complaints and Discipline branch, whose zest for rooting out rogue cops often bordered on the fanatic. They were a breed apart, the pariahs of the closed order of the police force, guarding their fat dossiers on the misdemeanours of their colleagues in triple-locked fireproof security cabinets on an upper floor of the glass and concrete blockhouse of the headquarters building where they nested like vultures.

Yes, he'd quite looked forward to meeting Vicky Rivers again, Royal thought bleakly, but now he wasn't so sure as he looked down at the file she had dumped between them. It was a thick bundle in a buff jacket heavily annotated and, by the look of it, the spade work had been completed and whatever odious investigation it contained was moving to a conclusion. What that might be, he could only guess, but more often than not a file of that magnitude meant one or more of their number would be required to don his best uniform and face a disciplinary trial in front of the Chief himself. *Quis custodes ipsos custodiet.* The growth industry.

Royal squinted despairingly at the bundle and breathed a sigh. 'You know, if it'd been anybody but you, I would've legged it out the back the minute I knew you were in the building,' he said gravely. 'You're going to ruin my reputation, you know that. Good old Bert Royal consorting with the scorpions who get a kick out of stinging decent coppers just because they did their jobs the best way they knew how.'

'By bending the rules,' Vicky replied tartly. 'Justice isn't a quick cough and a string of TICs on the sheet any more.

Can't pull strokes like that these days. We run the ESDA over the confession and find half the pages have been substituted for some fairy story. Don't tell me you condone that kind of thing?'

Royal felt a twinge of anger. The hotshots in the job, it was all black and white to them, by the manual. The old craft of thief-taking had all but died out. 'Listen, you get some time in, you're going to wonder about your precious rules and your fancy gadgets. I remember this case when I was on the squad with your father, girl found strangled in a churchyard, nice kid. The prime suspect was a Jesus freak—' he touched his temple— 'voices in the head, you know, but cunning as a fox. Wouldn't have it at any price until your old man put on a dog-collar, took him into the church and they prayed together. Got a full confession in the name of the Almighty.'

Vicky gave him a pained look. 'I've heard all the swashbuckling detective stories. They wouldn't wash these days and you know it. Even if you got it through the Crown Court, it'd be thrown out on Appeal.'

'More's the pity,' Royal said. 'At least we didn't have psychos walking the streets in those days. Your father locked 'em up and threw away the key. Nobody complained.'

Frowning slightly Vicky leaned forward and with the tips of her fingers pushed the file across the desk. She had no intention of getting sidetracked into reminiscences of the good old days.

'What's this?' Royal asked. He didn't touch the bundle.

'The Burton file,' Vicky said. 'The PCA have taken it under their wing.'

Royal pulled a face. The Police Complaints Authority, a bunch of do-gooders under a doddering retired judge who supervised investigations into police malpractice. What did they know about fighting for your life in some alley in the middle of the night while some maniac tried to bash your head in? 'Oh, wonderful,' he replied bleakly, 'they're bound to make a meal of it, and meantime I've got to run under strength with the crime rate going off the chart. Just what I needed.'

The Burton case was tragically simple. A silent intruder alarm had sent every unit within range to the Burton warehouse on a new business park beside the motorway. First on the scene were a couple of unit beat cars and the robbers had been caught red-handed loading a lorry in the compound. Eager to win their spurs, the officers had jumped in without back-up and a spirited fight had taken place during which heads had been cracked on both sides before reinforcements arrived and brought the situation under control. With only a thin defence to work on, the smart-alec lawyers had routinely instructed their clients to make complaints against the arresting officers, alleging they were innocent truck-drivers making an out of hours delivery when they were pounced upon, beaten up when they protested, and saddled with planted evidence and concocted confessions. It was all eyewash, of course, designed to provide a basis for an ambush defence in front of a jury, but the complaints procedure had moved smoothly into gear, the officers had been suspended and the rubber heels had started turning over the stones.

'Why're they so keen on this one?' Royal asked, still reluctant to touch the file lying in front of him.

'It's political,' Vicky said. 'I wouldn't be surprised if someone isn't stirring them up. A couple of MPs have got in on the act and the PCA's having kittens. They've got to be seen to be giving someone some stick, and this job just happened to come out of the hat.'

Appreciating the candour, Royal said, 'Well, I'm not saying my blokes are saints, and if I'd been there I wouldn't have jumped in with both feet like they did, but, Jesus Christ, they were good productive officers. How d'you think the rest of the shift's going to feel? Like looking the other way when they see a crime being committed, and who can blame 'em. Nicking villains isn't worth the candle any more, not if all you're going to get for it is a white form and your pension on the line.' He sighed. 'If you ask me, the whole world's turned upside down.'

'I just thought I'd bring you the news personally,' Vicky said, 'as you're the Sub-Divisional Commander. We're going to need their dockets and their annual reports, it's just routine.'

'Yeah, in a pig's eye,' Royal said. He could see the mud flying his way. Failure to exercise proper supervision. If the PCA really went to town he could come to grief too. His eyes fell to the file. 'What d'you want me to do with this?'

Vicky inspected her fingernails. 'I thought I might just forget to put it back in my case while I pop down to the ladies' and powder my nose. I'm not normally that careless.'

Royal smiled. 'What did I do to deserve such consideration?'

Vicky looked up, an artful expression on her face. 'For old times,' she said, 'and besides, one favour deserves another.' She delved into her briefcase and took out her pocket-book, flipping the pages until she found the notes she wanted. 'What can you tell me about a PC Bogan?'

CHAPTER 6

The kid was a carrot-top. Bogan spotted him as he walked down the mesh tunnel into the yard, flexing his knees into the well-lubricated strolling gait of the beat cop with time served. A lanky carrot-top with a shock of ginger hair and a wide-eyed expression on his face. He was wearing a yellow reflective jacket which made him look like a daffodil. 'Give me strength,' Bogan muttered to himself with mounting irritation. He liked to work alone, giving his instincts full rein, and for the most part the other old sweats on the station, the sergeants and inspectors, were happy to leave him to his own devices provided he turned in his quota of prisoners and process. Now he was going to have to break in a new popinjay of a sergeant, find his weakness and exploit it, so that he could get back into his old routine. It wouldn't be hard, he'd always found a way to get the eager beavers by the balls. Their hearts and minds invariably followed. But in the meantime he was saddled with Nigel Wilcox, the graduate with a head stuffed full of highbrow social theory, to cramp his style. If Bogan had his way they would recruit only milkmen into the job; at least they'd got some bottle and didn't mind getting wet.

He came out of the tunnel and walked over to where Wilcox was standing beside the Incident Car, a beat-up Montego estate with Day-Glo red fluorescent stripes down each side and a flasher across the roof which lit up like a Christmas tree.

'Just so we don't get off on the wrong foot, kid,' Bogan said, 'you do what I tell you and you don't give me a whole lot of backchat and maybe we'll rub along. I'm not your mother, your father or your wet-nurse, and I'm not going to pick you up and kiss it better if you come a cropper.

Long as we've got that straight you might just survive eight hours in this bathtub. Here endeth the first lesson.'

Without waiting for an answer he jerked open the driver's door and hauled himself into the sagging vinyl seat. Nigel hopped in from the other side, looking around the interior of the car in wonderment. A grille had been fitted at the back of the rear seats behind which was crammed an assortment of traffic cones, fold-up signs, ropes, tools and battery lamps to cater for any emergency.

'I'm really looking forward to this,' Nigel said. 'It's the first time I've been on the Incident Car. I've heard all about it, though, where the action is. You don't have to worry about me, I can take care of myself.' He leaned over the seat, peering into the back. 'As I'm the observer, do you want me to do the equipment check and note it in the log-book?'

'Forget it,' Bogan said. 'We're not going to be needing that junk.' He sniffed the rancid air and wrinkled his nose. The previous crew were two of the last great smokers and the ashtray was brimming with fag ends. 'You can chuck that lot out of the window, though.' He pointed at the ash tray. 'And leave it open, so we don't asphyxiate. Stinks in here like a Turkish wrestler's jockstrap.'

Bogan started up and swung the car out of the yard. Once they were on the road he picked up the radio handset which lay between the seats, pressed the talk button and said with studied boredom, 'Delta Romeo three-three, ten-one from Carpenter Road. Three-three out.' He clicked off without waiting for an acknowledgement, and turned the chatter from Delta Victor down to a murmur.

'You want me to monitor the radio?' Nigel asked.

'Be my guest,' Bogan said, 'if you like listening to that garbage. Only we won't be using it. The maggots have all got scanners.'

'Scanners?'

'Radio scanners,' Bogan said. 'Channel hoppers. Locks

on to our frequency so they can hear everything we're saying. Every villain worth his salt's got a scanner in his pocket these days.'

'I thought we had secure communications?'

Bogan laughed. 'Are you kidding? Last week a couple of DCs on the squad were staking out a suspect. Guy comes around the block riding in a dodgy motor, so they call in a PNC check. The guy comes around again, pulls up alongside, winds down the window and says, "Get it right, suckers, this is a turbo, not a GTI." That thing's worse than useless.' Bogan pointed at the UHF under the dashboard. 'You might as well be on the phone-in 'cause you're talking to the world.' He gave the carrot-top a sidelong glance. 'Look, kid, when you're working with me you only use the radio when you absolutely have to, understood? There's no way I'm giving the maggots the edge. The first time they know Ted Bogan's on to 'em is when I feel their collar.'

Nigel looked impressed at this piece of wisdom. He frowned. 'Isn't that an offence under the Wireless Telegraphy Act? We could do 'em for that.'

'Don't be a prat,' Bogan said. 'There's about a million laws we could do all sorts of people for all sorts of things, only they're all unenforceable. How long've you been in the job, Nige, six months?'

Nigel said, 'Be eight months next week.'

'Yeah, well, you can forget most of that crap they crammed into your head at training school. When you've been around as long as me, if you last that long, you'll get to know most of it isn't worth spit on the street. There's only one law the maggots understand, and that's Bogan's law.'

They were heading into town on the ring road when a beat-up Cortina jumped a red light and swerved in front of them. A youth grinned from the back seat and gave them the finger. Bogan flashed his headlights and blipped the siren. The Cortina accelerated, burning oil, but Bogan had no difficulty overtaking. He put on the flasher and the 'Police Stop' sign in the back window and pulled over, forcing the Cortina to stop.

'First process of the day,' he told Nigel gleefully. It was Bogan's habit to meet his process quota as early as possible into the shift, so that he didn't have to bother with the tedious chore later on.

'Shall I get a PNC check?' Nigel asked, looking in the rear-view mirror and noting the registration number.

'Nah,' Bogan said. 'They're not worth it. We've got 'em for jumping the light, that'll do for starters. Just stay here and watch my back.'

Bogan picked up his clipboard and got out of the Montego. He ambled casually towards the stationary Cortina, taking in the occupants. There were two youths and a girl inside, staring sullenly at him as he approached. All his senses sharpened. This was a dangerous moment, he knew that from long experience. The wildest things could happen on just such a routine pull as this and he'd known good cops get stabbed or shot while writing out a speeding ticket. As he came up to the driver's door the one behind the wheel rolled down the window. Bogan leaned in and his hand snaked inside and snatched the key from the ignition. The kid's eyes popped.

'OK, leadfoot.' Bogan stared him down. 'Where's the fire?'

'You can't do that,' the kid in the back piped up. 'What you stop us for?' He had on a green bandanna tied in a headband holding back a mane of dirty yellow hair.

Bogan pointed a finger at him. 'You, shut your mouth or you're nicked as well.' Then to the driver. 'You, out.'

The loudmouth in the back said, 'Don't you, Phil, we haven't done nothing.' He made a grunting sound and the girl beside him giggled.

Bogan ignored him. In a flat voice he told the driver, 'You want to listen to your friend, Phil, and get yourself into a lot of trouble, or you going to get this over with nice and easy? It's all the same to me.'

Bogan stepped back and reluctantly the kid got out of the car. A truculent scowl was forming on his face. 'Woody's right, I never done nothing. Why you hassling us? You got nothing better to do?'

'You jumped a red light back there. That's a moving traffic offence. Driving without due care at the very least. I could even bump it up to reckless. You get a summons, you go to court and you get fined a couple of hundred quid and lose your licence. Going to cramp your style, Phil.' Bogan stared into the kid's face as he moved him away from the car. He could see nerves ticking around the eyes and the mouth now that he'd cut him out from the pack, so he offered an alternative. 'But you look like a nice kid to me, Phil, so I tell you what. I could just write you a ticket and leave it at that. What d'you say?'

The kid shrugged. He glanced back at the Cortina where the others were making oinking noises. He was blinking rapidly and starting to sweat.

'Don't give me a hard time, son,' Bogan said. 'You jumped the light, right?'

The kid dropped his eyes. 'Yeah,' he muttered.

'I didn't catch that.'

'Yes,' the kid said, 'I thought I could make it.'

Bogan said, 'That'll do. You admit the offence. Now give me your driving licence.'

The kid took his wallet from the pocket of his jeans and handed over the licence. Bogan noted the details on the yellow fixed-penalty slip, signed it, tore it off and handed it to the kid. He walked him back to the car. 'Sounds like your playmates are bringing home the bacon,' he remarked.

'You going to give me my keys back?' the kid demanded, putting on a show of bravado.

'All in good time,' Bogan said. 'There's just one other

thing. Your tail-light's broken. Get it fixed or it's another ticket.'

'No, it's not,' the kid protested.

Bogan said, 'Oh yes it is, and it's a traffic hazard. You leave it like that, you're going to get pulled again. Look, I'll show you.'

Bogan took him around to the back of the car. The light clusters were intact. The kid stared at them. 'I told you they weren't bust,' he blurted, mystified.

With a flick of his wrist Bogan flipped the truncheon from its holster in a quick draw and delivered a sharp blow to the offside light cluster. The lens shattered and red and yellow fragments of plastic showered on to the road.

Bogan smiled. 'Didn't I tell you, smart-arse,' he said evenly. 'Now you be a good little boy and get it fixed or I'll do you again.' He handed back the ignition key. 'And next time I won't be so friendly. Now get this pigsty out of here.'

He watched them go and then walked back to the Montego.

'The maggots are out early,' he summed it up as he got back into the car.

'Why didn't we search their motor?' Nigel asked. 'They could have been going equipped?'

Bogan said, 'And if we'd found something?' He started the police car and pulled out into the traffic. 'We haul 'em back to the nick and go through the song and dance. They tell the custody officer to fuck off and scream for a brief while we twiddle our thumbs.' He drove one-handed. 'Some legal eagle breezes in quoting PACE ten to the dozen and even if we do get 'em to court they're out on bail before you can blink and we've wasted half a day bogged down in the paperwork.' Bogan hated the dreaded paperwork, and would go to enormous lengths to avoid the plethora of reports and statements which accompanied any arrest. But he did the only thing at which he was a past master: he committed Woody, the kid with the bandanna and the snake eyes, to his photographic memory. The wisdom of the street cop told him that he was the one to salt away for future reckoning.

'Either nick 'em in the act or forget it,' Bogan decreed. That way CID inherited the paperwork. 'Anything less, you're walking around in a legal minefield waiting for something to go bang. Law and Order, it's a joke. Nicking maggots isn't worth the candle.'

They circled around heading into town and Bogan rid himself of his quota of parking tickets on the reps' Sierras and Cavaliers choking the rat-runs between the brick terraces of Victorian villas which flanked the commercial district. Lazy buggers couldn't be bothered to use the car parks, they deserved to get stung. It was like shooting fish in a barrel. In the shopping centre Bogan swung the police car into the pedestrian area and cruised over the cobbles, resting his elbow on the open window. The Montego cut a swathe through the throng of lesser mortals.

'So tell me, Nige,' Bogan asked his new partner with a sneer in his voice, 'what'd you do at that fancy university of yours?'

Nigel was ready for the question. In the early days he had tried to answer it truthfully, but the only people with whom it had cut any ice were the recruiters, eager to snap up graduates. Now, as the first layers of cynicism had begun to harden, he didn't bother.

'The usual,' he replied, 'sex and drugs and rock'n'roll.'

Bogan waved to the girls behind the plate glass window of a travel shop. They waved back. He glanced across at the ginger-nut to see if he was joking. 'Oh yeah?'

Nigel knew that the horny old sweat was so steeped in prejudice that he would never comprehend the subtle delights of Milton's 'groves of Academe'. So he said, 'Randy birds, wall to wall, pick your own like strawberries.'

Bogan's interest was aroused. 'No kidding. You get plenty?'

'Different girl every week. Only the ripe ones, though.'

Bogan made the Montego swagger as he eased the car between the pedestrians. 'I didn't know you could get a degree in that?'

'Oh sure, they keep it dark, though. They call it Fine Arts. I got a second.'

'Sounds like the life.' Bogan was impressed. 'Not that I haven't had my share, but never that easy.'

Nigel said, 'My dad's a doctor, a GP. He wanted me to do medicine, but I couldn't face it. All I wanted to do was paint naked women. I was a big disappointment to my old man.'

Bogan almost hit a bollard outside Debenham's. 'You painted nudes?'

'What else? My thesis was on the contribution of pornography to modern art.'

'Jesus,' Bogan breathed, twisting the wheel to miss an elderly couple who weren't so spry on their feet. 'You'd got it made. So what're you doing in this lousy job?'

'I could've opened a gallery,' Nigel said, 'and gone bust inside a year, or taken myself off to a garret and painted stuff nobody wanted to buy. Only I couldn't find a rich widow pretty enough to be my patron.' He didn't enlighten Bogan on the cut-throat world of commercial art, or expand upon his minor contribution to the constructionalist theory of The Impressionists and the aching disillusion when his talent was not recognized. Instead he said, 'So I jacked it in, and here I am. Now I just paint for the hell of it.'

Bogan grinned. 'Still getting your leg over, though?'

'All the time,' Nigel said. 'Whenever I want.'

Suddenly a new dimension had opened up and Bogan began to warm to the carrot-top. 'No shit?' he said, hauling the Incident Car out of the pedestrian short cut and into the traffic-clogged High Street.

Nigel gave him a deadpan look as he recalled the response from his student days. 'Absolute constipation,' he replied.

CHAPTER 7

The first time Michael hit her was after the Commodore's party. Jojo was having trouble remembering things, getting the sequence right, but that episode was stuck in her memory and as it flooded back her legs began to feel weak with a tingling ache. She looked for somewhere to sit down, take a rest, and was surprised to see how far she had walked down the zigzag of pathways crisscrossing the bluff which sloped down to the Arrow Bridge. She had arrived at a small garden in the shape of a crescent cut into the hillside. There were benches and picnic tables, so she sat down to collect her thoughts and stop the pinwheel of fragmented memory from spinning out of control. Get herself together.

They had both been a little drunk, it was that kind of affair, Michael in his dinner jacket and she in a lime-green cocktail dress. All the swingers from the marina had been there, the yacht club set, topping each other with salty stories of their exploits on deep water. Then there was the Navy crowd from the shore base; officers in dress uniform and their bored wives displaying open contempt for the weekend sailors. One of them, a dark-haired matron showing her cleavage, paid Michael a lot of attention, not that Jojo really minded, she was having a good time herself. Circulate, Michael had told her, this kind of do was always good for contacts. And when she glanced across the room taking a breather from some amateur admiral's tall tales of intrepid seamanship, she was struck by how handsome Michael looked in formal clothes, the crisp white of his dress shirt setting off his diver's tan.

The Commodore's party was held in the Royal Yacht Club, a Gothic monstrosity on the waterfront with french windows which opened on to a sweeping terrace overlooking the marina and the inner harbour. After the buffet, a white-coated steward opened the glazed doors and the party spilled out on to the terrace to admire the twinkling riding lights of boats on the velvet blackness of the night. Jojo felt the chill of the breeze on her bare shoulders and went back inside to fetch her wrap. There was no sign of Michael among the knots of hardened drinkers still in the bars and buffet lounge.

Inside, the yacht club affected a nautical air of decks and cabins and as Jojo went up the sweeping staircase to the first floor, which was heavily panelled with pictures of ocean liners on the walls, she found she could not remember which of the quarterdeck cabins had been pressed into service as a ladies' cloakroom. She tried a door which opened under her hand. The room was in darkness, so she switched on the light and saw a couple copulating vigorously on the bed. The woman was the snooty Navy wife, her dress bunched up around her waist, blinking like a startled rabbit caught in the beam of a hunter's lamp as she peered over the black barathea shoulder of the man astride her. His face spun around, a blur which took on features terribly familiar. Michael's face contorted like a wild thing at bay.

Jojo flipped the switch, plunging the room back into darkness, stepped back and closed the door. Her mind had blanked out, refusing to accept the evidence of her eyes. She went back down in a daze and wandered around until Michael found her. He looked so normal as he took her arm, smiling and nodding to the other party guests, that for one frantic moment Jojo thought she had imagined it, a drink-induced hallucination, a panic nightmare.

His grip tightened on her elbow as he steered her out of there, took her to the car and drove home in silence. She was still in a trance when he pushed her into the flat, closed the door behind them and began systematically to beat her with short, sharp blows which filled her with pain. All she could see was his face floating in front of her eyes, puffed up with rage, the upper lip grotesquely swollen like the mottled throat of a bullfrog. Gratefully she was relieved of the anguish when she collapsed on the settee and passed out.

She was off work for two days. Michael acted as if nothing had happened, looking after her as though she had a bout of 'flu. But when she went back to the office with the bruises still showing Carol arched an eyebrow and said: 'What happened? You walk into a bus or something?'

Jojo said it was just stupid, she'd fallen and hurt herself. No bones broken, luckily. Carol said, 'Yeah, I've seen that kind of fall before. You just sort of trip and fall on to a fist.' It wasn't anything like that, Jojo said, but she couldn't look her friend in the eyes. Carol said, 'Well, it's your business, and I'd be the last one to interfere, but when you want a good solicitor let me know. The bastard does that to you again, you want to take him for everything he's got. One thing about my old man, the snooker champ, he knows if he lays a finger on me, it's going to be a replay of the Crucifixion and I'll be going for the maximum break. Remember what I told you before: when you get right down to it, all men are double-dyed bastards.'

Jojo sat in the picnic place and stared at the sleek lines of the Arrow Bridge straddling the river. Take him for everything he'd got, that was a joke. She had never pried into Michael's business affairs, she was just happy that the diving school appeared to be doing so well, and they had everything they wanted. When Michael said they were on their way to making their first million, milking the punters who wanted to learn to swim with the fishes, she believed him. Clothes with designer labels, eating out at swank restaurants, the flat furnished from the pages of *Lifestyle* magazine. Nothing but the best.

At first Jojo told herself that the incident at the Commodore's party had been a freak occurrence, a twist of human nature for which she blamed herself. Maybe she had denied

Michael something he craved. Some thrill, some excitement she couldn't supply. He became so solicitous afterwards that her theory seemed more and more credible, but a nagging doubt remained, and one day, feigning a headache, she left work early, returned to the flat and went through the room he used as a study. She felt like a thief in the night, riffling through the jumble of paperwork stuffed into the drawers of his desk. Guilt gave way to sick panic as she discovered the rags to riches story was a myth, a cruel joke. Instead of the fortune Michael had promised, the bank statements told a story of crippling debts. Even the flat had been remortgaged to stave off the bailiffs, and the dunning demands for long unpaid bills ran into figures which looked like telephone numbers. They were drowning in debt, and with her easy acceptance of Michael's outward charm, the gold bracelets, the Armani suits, the Rolex and the Jaguar, she had been unaware of the fact that they were stony broke and going down for the third time. She sat for a long time with her head in her hands, wondering if she was going mad and it was all a nightmare from which she would awake. Then she dried her eyes, took a shower, replaced everything as she had found it, put on fresh make-up and her favourite turquoise shell suit and went for a long walk.

But for some strange reason nothing seemed familiar any more. She walked up to town, but the stores with their beckoning window displays seemed to be mocking her. All at once she felt trapped in an alien place, and without thinking she jumped on to a passing bus, not even bothering to check its destination. When she got off, fifteen minutes later, feeling calmer and not a little foolish, she looked around to get her bearings and realized that she was on Marine Drive. Feverishly she searched for a landmark, something to hang on to, and her eyes settled on the one feature which stood out from the riverside sprawl. The Arrow Bridge. Jojo stared at the bridge and closed her eyes.

She counted to ten and opened them again. The bridge was still there, solid and dependable.

Mechanically she began walking towards the bridge when a horn sounded behind her, two light notes to attract her attention, and she saw a Toyota Hi-Lux cut out of the evening rush-hour traffic streaming down the Drive and angle in to the kerb. A familiar face was looking out of the cab of the pick-up.

'Jojo? It *is* you! I thought it was you, but I couldn't be sure, so I took a chance. Gee, I'm glad it is you, could've had my face slapped or worse, could've got myself reported for kerb-crawling.' The face split into a laugh and then grew serious. 'Hey, Jojo, you all right? You look like you've seen a ghost.'

Behind the John Lennon glasses she recognized Gary Summers, a small-time builder who made his living buying up and renovating the little terraced houses which passed through the books of the estate agency. He made a habit of dropping in at the office at least once a week to see if there was anything new he could snap up cheap, and as Jojo handled most of the repossessions and executors' sales, they had become acquaintances and then friends. He would bring her small tokens, chocolates or perfume, and she knew that he was fond of her and there would be awkward moments between them when he asked her out and she turned him down.

'Oh hello, Gary,' she replied, making an effort to sound cheery. 'No, I'm fine, just out for a breath of fresh air.'

'Well, all you're going to breathe here is carbon monoxide,' Gary said, leaning across the seat of the pick-up to the open passenger's window. 'Hop in. I want to show you something.'

'Gary, I can't.' She made a show of looking at her watch. 'I've got to get home. Michael'll wonder where I've got to.'

'It'll only take a minute,' Gary said. 'Anyway it's business really, I just wanted to show you the house in Churchill

Street I've been doing up. You remember, the one that was falling down? It's a little palace now. Come on, hop in.'

Jojo was shaking her head, about to brush him off, when she thought: What the hell, and instead she produced a smile and crossed the pavement to the Toyota. 'As long as it's only a minute. You promise?'

'I promise, cross my heart.' Gary made the sign on his workshirt to reassure her, grinning from ear to ear. 'I just thought you'd like to see the result of our hard bargaining for once. Help you recommend me to future clients when you see what a good job I've done.'

He pushed open the door and Jojo climbed into the pick-up. 'You don't have to prove anything to me, Gary,' she said. 'If you were a cowboy or a jerry-builder, I wouldn't be selling you houses.'

'Yeah,' Gary replied, gunning the Hi-Lux back into the traffic, ''cause if you were a hard bitch estate agent, I wouldn't be buying 'em from you.'

Jojo leaned back against the seat, grateful for the diversion. Her mind had been running out of control like a flywheel about to spin off its axis and shatter into a million fragments. The shock of Michael's duplicity had hit her like a hammer blow, but as she came to terms with that, a second horror had enveloped her. How could Michael have spent so much money so quickly? Where had it all gone? Sitting in the truck listening to Gary chatter on about his prowess as a master craftsman, she summoned the mental energy to struggle free from the waves of black despair which had all but engulfed her. All the same, she dreaded finding out.

Now, sitting in the picnic place, staring at the bridge, she almost wished she could hear the toot of Gary's horn again and he would be there to whisk her away once more. There had been no comfort and joy in finding out, she knew that now that it was all over. Idly she wondered if things would have turned out differently if she had not taken a ride with

Gary Summers that day, but she dismissed the thought as too painful to contemplate. Instead she got up and continued her walk down the pathway towards the one constant anchor which never changed. The Arrow Bridge.

CHAPTER 8

Bogan was warming to the carrot-top. As they cruised around the town's main streets, showing the flag, he thought maybe he could make something of the kid after all. Nigel wasn't so bad for a graduate, not like some of the woodentops he'd been obliged to work with in the past, heads stuffed full of do-gooder sociology and spouting the manual every time he tried to give them an object lesson in streetcraft. At least Nigel was respectful and willing to learn. Bogan began to think that maybe he had been a little hasty in his sweeping condemnation of the breed. It was just possible that Nigel would make a halfway decent copper in the end.

Watching the streets drift by, Nigel felt the same stirrings of affinity for his new crewmate. Although he still had more than half his probation to go before he could hope to be confirmed in the office of constable, Nigel Wilcox was already succumbing to the allure of the beat. Walking the streets in the uniform gave him a buzz which, despite his university education, he found impossible to put into words. Balzac had tried, describing the policeman as an amalgam of artist, priest and soldier, and Nigel, harking back to that romantic age, found the analogy entirely satisfactory. Not that he would have dared venture such a flowery opinion among his peers, with whom a coarse barrack room vocabulary was the common conversational currency. Yet he felt it just the same. The uniform transformed him into someone to be counted on, a person of substance, yet at the same time imbued with the raffish devil-may-care of an adventurer taking a tilt at life's windmills. Whenever he returned to his student haunts for a few drinks with his contemporaries he would deflect the half-serious taunts that he had defected to the Praetorian Guard of the Establishment with a knowing smile and a shake of his head. Maturity was settling on his shoulders and he was determined to show these latter-day radicals who had opted for safe careers as accountants and computer programmers that of the young blades who once caroused on the sprawling campus of that redbrick university, a spark still burned in the breast of Nigel Wilcox.

So he recounted the cops-and-robbers stories overheard in the canteen, and soon held his audience enthralled. It had not been so when they were students, when Nigel, a solitary soul, absorbed in his studies, had shown no talent for the excesses of college life. There were miserable moments when he tried and failed, none so awful as that rag week when the pranksters hauled an effigy of the Vice Chancellor on to the ramparts of the Victorian administration building and gleefully drew straws for the honour of scaling the clock tower to perch their guy on the highest pinnacle. Swept along by their madcap scheme, Nigel drew the short straw and, unable to pull back despite the vertigo which immediately seized him, gritted his teeth and began to climb the tower. The next thing he remembered was opening his eyes to find himself sprawled on the cot in his room, the others gathered around him. Without bothering to disguise their disgust, they recounted in cruel detail how he had wet himself, frozen on a ledge far from the summit; how they had had to pull his pathetic hide back down to safety. A catatonic trance: one of the medics had sneered a diagnosis as they broke out six-packs and squirted him with beer, his ignominy complete.

Then there was the smouldering resentment of his father to be endured. Frank Wilcox, a hulking practical man with calloused hands and a perplexed expression who earned his living as a central heating engineer, had little in common with his long-haired offspring who was always more at home with sketchpad and pastels than a pipe wrench.

Groping for a father-and-son accommodation, Frank began to take inordinate pride in the fact that he had sired the intellectual of the family, bragged about it in the pub after work. The young Michelangelo who would one day redecorate the Sistine Chapel, no less.

When Nigel threw it all up and took the graduate entrants' test for the police force, Frank was mortified. Confess to his mates that his genius of a son had become a hated copper! He'd sooner cut off his right hand.

Recognizing the pain of betrayal in his old man's eyes, Nigel did the decent thing and put distance between himself and his family, secure in his belief in the recruiter's pledge as he sailed through the extended interview that he was on the fast track to promotion and a chief constable's baton was already in his knapsack. One day the prodigal would return and his father's chest would once more swell with pride.

But these sacrifices were as nothing compared with the seduction of the beat, and to crew for Ted Bogan, the maestro himself, was something to be savoured. As he studied his tutor out of the corner of his eye, Nigel imagined himself the colt learning the ways of the stallion. He felt quietly elated.

After a while Bogan pulled the Montego into a service road between the concrete and glass monoliths of the department stores, swung into the mouth of a loading area displaying No Waiting signs, and shut off the engine.

'That'll do for the magical mystery tour,' he told his partner seriously. 'All that riding around all day in this tin can'll do for you is give you piles, curse of the traffic lads who're too idle to get off their fat backsides. You want to do the real job, Nige, you've got to get out and about on your feet. Time we shook some doorknobs.'

Bogan picked up the radio-phone and told Delta Victor that they were going ten-one on foot patrol and switching to channel eight UHF on their personal radios. He clicked off without waiting for the dispatcher's response.

They walked down Lombard Street where the stores rubbed shoulders with high rise office buildings and strolled into the Ocean Wave shopping plaza where Bogan was soon in his element, exchanging gossip with the shopkeepers, flirting with the girl assistants, and generally making everyone feel good to see the uniform. Nigel found himself sucked along in the vortex of banter which Bogan generated around himself. Everybody from the store detectives to the old boy who pushed a mechanical sweeper across the malls seemed to want to bend his ear, and Nigel was impressed at the ease with which his partner could slip in and out of conversations, always giving the impression that nothing else mattered. Perhaps Bogan wasn't such a dinosaur after all.

Emerging from the freeze-dried air-conditioning of the plaza, they stood on the street corner and watched the four lanes of traffic on the one-way system ebb and flow.

'Now could you ever imagine such a pleasant way to spend a morning,' Bogan remarked, feeling good. 'Meet nice people, pass the time here and there, chat up the birds, and they even pay us to have such a good time.'

'Must be a quiet day,' Nigel said. 'We didn't get a single shout.'

Bogan smiled. 'That's why we're here. It's a radio dead spot, they'll never raise us here.'

Nigel looked surprised. 'Aren't we supposed to—'

But Bogan cut him off. 'Come on, nightrider,' he said. 'There's a whole lot more to police work than jumping around on the end of a chain. Let's get on with your education, all this yakking's making me thirsty. Time we had a coffee-break.'

He steered Nigel into The Halyard, a narrow, cobbled street crammed with boutiques. 'You're in torpedo alley now, Nige.' He pointed out the little shops, their traditional façades fashioned from plaster mouldings and bull's eye glass. 'You go in there—' he pointed out a hair stylists called Bosun's—'you'll be forking out seven-fifty for a trim and you either get a tit or a dick in your face, depending on your preference.' He walked on. 'You want a nice silk shirt, go and see Jeremy in The Locker over there.' He pointed out a fashion shop. 'Only take a tip from me, that bum bandit gets you in the dressing-room, you'd better keep your back tight to the wall.'

Over a striped awning reminiscent of the Mediterranean, a sign read Gina's Frocks. 'Our coffee-stop,' Bogan announced, pushing open the door and leading Nigel inside. The narrow shop was crammed with racks of pastel-coloured dresses packed in so tight there was hardly room to move around.

'Gina!' Bogan called out. 'Police! It's a raid.'

The woman appeared from the back of the shop, a smile spreading across her face. 'Ciao, Teddy,' she replied cheerfully. 'You come to take me away from all this?' She came around the racks. She had squeezed herself into black Lycra jodhpurs and wore a billowy white silk organza shirt under which her breasts disported without the restriction of a bra.

'Gina, this is Nigel.' Bogan made the introductions. 'You know how you tell a genuine Italian lady, Nige? They don't shave under their arms.'

Gina gave him a playful slap and he caught her wrist. 'Assaulting a police officer, eh?' he joked. 'And in front of a witness too.'

'You deserve it,' Gina said, 'back home in Italy, it's the other way around. The Carabinieri assault the pretty girls. My bottom was always black and blue.'

'Nice work if you can get it,' Bogan said. 'When we go into Europe, maybe I'll get myself a transfer.'

Gina said, 'Long as it's only my bottom you pinch, Teddy.'

Laughing, Bogan turned to Nigel. 'Isn't she something?

I'll never get a better proposition than that.' He returned his attention to the woman, still holding her wrist where the cuff of her shirt was fastened with a jet stud. 'Why don't you put the kettle on, Gina. We could have a cappuccino while I give that some thought.'

They drank coffee in the cramped back room, still teasing each other, and then Gina said, 'You want to see what I've done with the upstairs, Teddy? It's going to be my beauty salon.'

'Sure,' Bogan said, letting Gina take him by the hand. He winked at Nigel. 'You want to mind the shop a minute, Nige? You might meet that rich widow you were on about.'

He followed Gina up the stairs into a big loft which had been freshly painted but as yet contained no furniture. A large bay window overlooked the street. No sooner were they alone than Gina drew him against her, her pearly pink lips parting a little breathlessly. 'Take me away, Teddy,' she murmured in his ear, nibbling the lobe. 'We can go to my villa at Bordighera, it's warm there. We can drink *caffè freddo* at a little place I know and make love among the flowers.'

She pressed herself against him urgently and Bogan could feel the heat of her breasts through the designer silk.

'Your old man wouldn't like that, princess,' he said. 'Probably have some Mafia capo chop off my balls.'

'Forget Massimo,' Gina sighed. 'His blood is like ice. All he thinks about is his stupid business.' She took his face in her hands and kissed him, tilting her pelvis into his. Idly, Bogan wondered why he seemed to attract wealthy women. The boutique was just a hobby for Gina, her old man had made a pile peddling frozen pizzas to supermarkets. Then there was rich bitch Maddie on the boat who couldn't get enough of him. A random thought almost made him laugh out loud. Maybe it wasn't him at all. Maybe they just had a uniform fetish. But whatever his charm, he reflected ruefully, it cut no ice with Iris, the nine-to-five working girl who spat in his face every time he tried to patch up their marriage. When he got near a phone he'd give her another call, just on the off-chance of catching her at an unguarded moment. But in the meantime there was a slice of real Italian pizza on offer and Bogan was never one to pass up an opportunity. Gina was hanging around his neck, working on his ear with the tip of her tongue. Bogan reached down and undid the button at the waist of her sleek designer jodhpurs and began to feel for the zipper. Looking over her shoulder, out of the window, he watched the traffic snarl up at the end of the street. Around the corner of Marks and Spencer a yellow Jaguar XJS convertible, the white hood down, nosed out of the flow and turned into The Halyard. Bogan watched the car approach and as it passed he recognized the driver. It was the little creep he'd had a run-in with at the marina that morning. His eyes narrowed as he disengaged himself from the embrace, took out a ballpoint and jotted the registration on the back of his hand.

'Bogan?' Bert Royal repeated the name, careful to conceal the new twinge of alarm. 'Yeah, he's one of mine.' He made the admission carefully, for with two hundred and fifty officers under his command, he usually had difficulty putting a face to a name. But Bogan popped up clear as crystal, overweight, truculent, burned out, yet still a crafty street cop with nowhere else to go. For some reason, just saying his name sent a shiver up Royal's spine. 'What's he been up to?'

Vicky Rivers, her make-up freshened, reached across the desk, picked up the bulky Burton file and stuffed it into her briefcase. She closed the clasps, set the Samsonite to one side and leaned forward. 'Can we make this confidential?'

Royal picked up a rubber band from the pile of clutter in front of him and began to wind it around his fingers. 'Do I have a choice?'

'Of course. If you say no dice, I will smile sweetly, thank

you for the coffee, and leave you wondering just what the hell Jack Rivers's little girl is up to.'

The rubber band stretched between his fingers. 'And if I agree?'

'Then I'll trust you to keep this between the two of us. A conversation which never happened.'

'This wouldn't be one of the Deputy's little party pieces, would it? He didn't send you here to wind me up by any chance?'

She shook her hair. 'Oh no, this is all mine. Nobody else knows a thing about it. I didn't put it in the log, and you know why? They'd've just patted me on the head and given it to one of the boys. I don't intend that to happen.'

Royal stretched the band taut. Under the rigid rules of the complaints procedure every investigation had to be dutifully recorded. The Deputy Chief and the humourless martinet of a Chief Superintendent who ran the branch were sticklers for the formalities. Surely Vicky knew that. 'His nibs'll skin you alive when he finds out.'

Her cheeks reddened and the blush seeped down the curve of her neck into her cleavage. When she spoke she was slightly breathless. 'Hear me out, Uncle Bert, before you read me the Riot Act. I'm going to tell you something now, something I've never mentioned to anybody before . . . so you'll understand why I'm doing this.' Her brows knitted in thought. 'Your friend Jack Rivers, the great CID legend, was a monster.'

Royal felt a twinge of embarrassment at the earnest way she said that. He got up from the desk and went back to the easy chair, her eyes following him. 'Vicky—' he fiddled with the rubber band—'you don't have to—'

She waved a hand. 'Oh yes I do. At home he treated Mum like a skivvy and me like dirt. He was a man's man and women irritated him. He hated me because I wasn't the boy he always wanted, and most of the time we lived in awe of him, never knowing when he was going to come in or go out.'

She paused and drew breath. 'He was never a father, but all the same he fascinated me. I watched him and I listened to him, and despite him, I learned from him. When you and the rest of his cronies came around to the house, drinking and playing cards and talking shop, I used to sit on the stairs and listen to you going on about your beloved police force and one lesson came home to me: it doesn't matter how talented or experienced you are, the only way you'll get on in the job is if you're in the right place at the right time and your face fits. And if you wait for that to happen, you can wait until hell freezes. You have to make your own luck.'

'Oh, come on,' Royal murmured, afraid of where this soul-bearing might lead. 'That's pretty cynical.'

Her eyes blazed suddenly. 'Tell me it isn't true! You have to be a woman in a man's world to really appreciate the subtlety.' She tossed her hair. 'Oh, I used to believe in fair play, equal opportunities. I did all the courses, detective basic and advanced, HOLMES, hostage negotiator, top marks on all of 'em, they couldn't fault me. I passed the inspector's exam with flying colours while I was a WPC, but I was still the last on the select list to get the rank and when they turned me down for CID I decided to play them at their own game. Wheedled my way into headquarters by going all out for a job nobody wanted, a rubber heel rooting out the rotten apples, and now I'm right under their noses where they can't ignore me.' The angry flush on her face deepened. 'And I'm playing dirty 'cause that's the only way the men who run this outfit like their own private club are going to sit up and take notice. And you're going to help me make my luck stick.'

Royal watched the fire blaze with dismay. What had happened to that tomboy of a girl he had known all those years ago? Had she really become this shrew, embittered by beating her head against the wall of a male preserve? Jesus, he hoped not, but all the indications were there, and as his eyes fell to the notebook open on her lap, his thoughts turned to self-preservation. Whatever she was up to, he didn't want her careering around his town like a loose cannon. He nodded slowly. 'You'd better tell me about it, Vicky, then we'll see. Only you're taking a risk. How'd you know I'm not one of the boys, part of the male conspiracy? How'd you know you can trust me?'

A bright smile transformed her face. 'Because you're my good old Uncle Bert.'

Royal sank back, stretching the band between his fingers. 'You mentioned Bogan. Where does he fit into this?'

A crafty look crossed her face. 'Bogan's my meal ticket.' She looked down at her scribbled notes, gathering her thoughts. Then she said, 'I'll lay it out for you. They gave me the ends of the Burton thing to tie up, a little clerical chore to keep me happy, but I bumped into this guy, Armstrong, Terry Armstrong, partner in a security firm called Baywatch. He started running off at the mouth about how his best clients weren't renewing their contracts. Oh, at first he put it down to the recession, everybody tightening their belts a notch, but then he started asking around and discovered it wasn't any such thing. He was being undercut by somebody else muscling in on his customers. So he did some digging and guess what he came up with?'

'Amaze me,' Royal replied, not wanting to hear what was coming.

'A new face hustling a bargain offer. So I checked it out with the Chamber of Trade, no trace. Then I got Armstrong to put the word around and you know what he turned up?'

Royal stretched the band, watched the rubber quiver. 'I get the feeling I'm not going to like this.'

'A blue suit.'

Royal nodded.

'Named Bogan. Offering personal service. Cut-price

security for a backhander out of the petty cash. That's an offence under the discipline code.'

'Always assuming you can prove it.'

'Oh, I will. With your help. I intend to sit on friend Bogan like his shadow, catch him with his hand in the till and hang his sorry hide out to dry.'

Royal wagged his head. 'If you're right, and it's a big if, you're going to need a lot more than circumstantial. Be a tough nut to crack, Vicky. Bogan's got a lot of time in, he's not stupid.'

'So tell me about him.'

'What's to tell? Twenty years on the beat, that about covers it. Done some good work in his time, as I recall, a few commendations to show for it. A street cop.' He toyed with the rubber band. 'The kind your old man appreciated. If I'd got a dozen like him instead of the kids they're sending me these days straight out of training school . . .' He left the sentiment there and met her eyes. 'Look, Vicky, you sure you're not barking up the wrong tree on this? Bogan's a good man, I'd hate to lose him.'

Her eyes blazed. 'Don't tell me you condone this? We're talking gross misconduct here, conduct likely to bring the force into disrepute. I'm going to nail him and hand him to the Dep on a plate, with or without your help.'

Royal winced. 'If you're right he'll be gone anyway. Sounds like he's got a head start on government policy, privatize police services, probably end up in the Home Office planning unit. Sounds like their kind of guy.'

She gave him a withering look and Royal waved a hand in weary acquiescence. 'Only joking, Inspector,' he said, 'How do you want to play it?'

'Help me tail him,' she said. 'If my information's right, today's the day he collects the grocery.'

Royal slumped back in his chair and stretched the strip of rubber between his fingers. Without warning the band snapped.

CHAPTER 9

The counter boy looked as if he was in astronaut training. He wore headphones clamped over his beanie with a microphone on a stalk which jiggled in front of his mouth as he came out with the standard lines: 'Good morning, sir, how may I serve you?'

Paul said, 'Give me a quarter-pounder with everything and double fries.' He turned to look for Russ and saw him coming in through the door. 'What're you having?' Paul called out, and Russ insinuated himself in to the head of the queue at the counter, ignoring the glowering looks. 'Cheeseburger,' he said, studying the gaudy overhead display. 'Yeah, cheeseburger'll do me.'

'And a cheeseburger,' Paul told the junior astronaut who was already relaying the order into the mike and playing a tune on the plastic-sealed register. 'Anything to drink, sir?' he asked.

'Chocolate shake,' Paul said. He looked at Russ. 'Uh, coffee,' Russ said. They picked up their snack on a plastic tray and took it to one of the tables. When they were seated Paul said, 'OK, Nigel Mansell, just what the hell d'you think you were playing at, giving that thing some wellie? You almost rammed me a couple of times. And what the Christ were you doing with the hood? It was going up and down like a yo-yo?'

'It's full of buttons,' Russ said. 'You can't tell which does what. You touch the pedal and the thing takes off. You press something and the windows go up and down and the hood shoots off. You should've told me it was complicated, I'd have taken a course.'

'All you had to do was drive it,' Paul said, taking a bite out of his burger. 'You're not entered for Silverstone or anything. The bits you don't understand you leave well alone.'

Russ said, 'I'm a Morris Minor man. I drive by the seat of my pants.' He leaned forward. 'I tell you something, though.' He paused for effect, 'There's a knife in that car.'

'A what?'

'A knife. In the Jag. It's rolling around the floor, and you know what?' He left the question hanging for a second and then said, 'Looks like it's got blood on it.'

Paul was not impressed. He took a pull on his shake. 'You know your trouble, Russ?' he said. 'You've got an overactive imagination. Don't wind me up, I'm not in the mood. We've just snatched back the banana split and we're taking it in to make Ron's day, remember? That's the whole story. So don't go giving me any knives or blood or any of that private eye fantasy stuff you've got on the brain, not today, OK?'

Russ shrugged. 'See for yourself. I didn't touch it, it's still in the motor.'

'Talking of which,' Paul said, 'where did you park it?'

'Just around the corner,' Russ answered. 'You nicked the last space out front. I had to go around the block.'

Paul sighed. He wiped grease from his chin with a paper napkin. 'You're not safe to be out on your own, you know that? You'd better give me the keys. I'll take it the rest of the way.'

Russ felt in his pocket and a sheepish expression formed on his face. 'I must've left 'em in the car, I was in a hurry.'

'Oh, wonderful,' Paul said, cramming the last of the quarter-pounder into his mouth and washing it down with thick cold chocolate. 'You know what I ought to do? I ought to have you certified.'

A battered Cortina with a broken rear light cluster came around the corner for the second time and eased up alongside the yellow XJS Convertible which was inexpertly parked at the kerb. From the back seat the green bandanna made a twirling motion with a forefinger, indicating to the driver to go around the block again. The Cortina moved off.

'Good morning, Vietnam,' Woody exclaimed. 'Got to be my birthday. Silly sod even left the keys in.'

Phil said, 'Jesus, Woody, you having me on? What if that copper took my number?'

'He's lost his bottle,' the girl said, putting on a sing-song voice, her hand caressing the inside of Woody's thigh.

'Shut your face, Sonia,' Woody told her. 'This is between me and him.' He leaned forward, resting an arm on the back of the passenger's seat. 'He wanted, he would've got your number when he stopped us. Lucky for him he was too lazy to turn us over, otherwise I would've had to do him right there and then.'

'He's wetting himself,' the girl sneered.

Woody turned on her, his snake eyes hooded. 'I told you to shut it. Any more lip and I'll shut it for you.'

'Charming,' the girl muttered, removing her hand and flopping back in the seat.

'So what's it going to be, Phil?' Woody wanted to know. 'You got the balls for this, or do I have to fly it solo?'

Phil said, 'That bastard bust my light. I wish you had done him.'

Woody read the signs. Phil was psyching himself up. He'd be all right in a minute. 'He tries that again, you can do him yourself.' He reached down into the sports bag between his feet, took out the sawn-off and tapped Phil on the arm. Phil glanced down at the stubby shotgun. 'Meanwhile, Buckeye, we get our chance to stick some fat pigs just the way we planned it. Rip off some serious money. So what's it going to be? Are you in or are you chickening out?'

Phil concentrated on his driving. They were coming around again, turning into the street where the yellow Jaguar was parked. He swallowed nervously, glanced in the mirror. The girl in the back gave him a Madonna pout, and in that instant he wanted more than anything to be like Woody, grabbing everything and not giving a toss. They were coming up on the Jag again and he knew it was now or never. He steeled himself. 'Let's do it,' he said.

Woody had the back door open as they came alongside the XJS. He slipped out, took two quick paces and vaulted over the door into the seat, reached forward and turned on the engine. The Jaguar slid out of the parking space and fell in behind the Ford. Inside the Cortina the girl took Woody's place against the seat back and whispered a promise into Phil's ear.

Two young men in sports shirts came around the corner at a fast trot. Russ skidded to a stop and stared in disbelief at the empty space where he had parked the Jaguar. 'I don't believe it,' was all he could say.

Paul swung round on him. 'Don't tell me what I think you're going to tell me. If you value your miserable life, don't tell me.'

'I don't believe it,' Russ repeated, looking up and down the street, then back at the empty stretch of kerb. 'I left it right here, and now it's gone!'

Paul grabbed a handful of shirt and threw Russ back against the wall. 'I ought to crack your skull, you dummy. He must've followed us and you left it for him on a plate. You know what he's done? He's snatched back the snatchback.'

Russ's eyes widened. 'You think that's what happened?'

Paul let go and began to beat his fists against the wall.

Bogan didn't waste much time looking for the yellow Jaguar. He cruised the Montego up and down the main streets which surrounded The Halyard checking the cars parked on the meters and left it at that. He could easily have radioed for a PNC check on the registration number scrawled on the back of his hand, but that would have alerted the Operations Room to his position and availability and he knew from experience that once they had him on the air the operators would begin shovelling work his way, and getting tied up on domestics and footling inquiries was something he intended to avoid. Instead he preferred to rely on his intuition, which told him that sooner or later the Jag would turn up again. All he had to do was be patient.

They left the town and drove down through the docks, emerged from a Legoland industrial estate and swung on to Marine Drive. Up ahead the Arrow Bridge spanned the river.

'I hate to mention this,' Nigel said, 'but aren't we off our sector?'

'When you've got the Incident Car, you don't have a sector,' Bogan explained. 'We're free as the breeze, Nige. We go where we want, fighting crime, righting wrongs, giving the public their money's worth. We're the top team on this shift, so we keep on our toes, ready for the big one. Leave the panda jockeys to shovel up the rubbish.'

Nigel felt uneasy. After the briefing at the station, when he was told he would be riding with Bogan, Sergeant Davies had taken him to one side and in a conspiratorial tone had instructed him to keep a close watch on the old buzzard and report anything unusual back to him personally, particularly if Bogan tried to sneak down to the Arrow Bridge which was off their beat. He didn't elaborate and now Nigel was torn by a conflict of loyalty. He couldn't afford to alienate the sergeant who had the power of God over a probationary constable yet he didn't want to betray his newfound mentor. Watching the low aluminium-clad warehouses of the container port slide past, he decided to try a little subtlety.

Leaning forward, he turned up the police radio. The

chatter filled the car. 'Did you hear that? Isn't that our call sign? That's the third time they tried to get us.'

Bogan leaned across and lowered the volume. 'No point in listening to that thing down here. Transmission's breaking up so bad it could be anything. What d'they expect? They give us this crap for radio sets, I can't hear a thing through that mush.'

'Shall I try to raise 'em on another channel?' Nigel's unease was deepening. 'We could be missing a decent shout. It's worth a try.' He reached for the handset, but Bogan stopped him. 'Forget it,' he said. 'These Micky Mouse radios are worse than useless. We'll report it's on the blink when we go in for meal break.'

Bogan circumnavigated a roundabout on the bridge approach and turned into the Trade Winds, an out of town supermarket which sported a replica of a clipper ship over the glass and steel entrance. The plastic sails of the three-master billowed as if under a stiff sou'wester and the perspective created the illusion of the ancient trader about to run on to the grey steel tangle of the bridge superstructure which reared up close by, dwarfing the squat cuboid shape of the store's corrugated slab walls adorned with post-modernist fripperies fashioned from hoops of scarlet tubing which supported the glazed walkways. Wire shopping trolleys had been abandoned haphazardly around the car park and youths in green overalls bearing the Trade Winds logo were herding them into trains and threading the metal snakes between the parked cars and back into the glass maw of the store.

Bogan drove down the lines of family saloons and hatchbacks parked in neat rows between the white lines of the checkerboard and stopped beside a low brick rectangle containing shrubs, from which sprouted a slender pole hung with a grapelike cluster of globe lights. He switched off and told Nigel, 'Sit tight and keep your eyes peeled. Couple of housewives got mugged for the loose change in their handbags the other day, right here in broad daylight.' He reached into the back for his anorak and opened the car door, shrugging the civvy coat over his uniform, leaned back in and said, 'I'm going to make a crime prevention call.'

Before Nigel could protest, Bogan was gone, striding towards the low frontage of the store. Nigel watched him go with a fresh pang of anxiety. If this was official police business, why had his partner so deliberately concealed his uniform? He glanced around, hoping that something would explain Bogan's odd behaviour, and watched a bronze Cavalier swing into the car park and slip into a vacant slot across from the entrance to the Trade Winds just as the glass doors opened and Bogan disappeared inside. Consumed with his own doubts, Nigel didn't give the Cavalier a second glance as he pondered Bogan's valediction. Crime prevention call! He sank down in his seat and began to grin to himself. Pulling another bird more likely. Even on brief acquaintance, he was getting the strong impression that no female was safe from the amorous advances of Ted Bogan. He heaved a sigh and prepared to sit it out, the police radio still droning its litany from the speaker. With nothing else to do he eavesdropped on the clipped exchanges between the radio room and the patrol units and after a while he reached down and fingered the handset resting in its cradle, itching to call in, to become part of the action. But although his conscience troubled him, loyalty stayed his hand. Whatever else he might be, Bogan was his crewmate and he couldn't let him down. Nigel sank deeper into his seat, folded his arms and gave up thinking about it.

In the Cavalier, Bert Royal switched off the engine and gave Vicky a despairing glance. He knew from the gleam in her eye just what was coming and he didn't relish it one bit. I'm too long in the tooth for this kind of caper, he told himself bleakly as he wished for the millionth time as they trailed the Incident Car around the city that his old pal Jack Rivers had had a son he could deal with man to man, instead of this firebrand of a daughter out to prove to the world that she was better than anything in trousers. He almost groaned out loud. Vicky Rivers was already twisting him around her little finger, and here he was waiting for the chance to pounce on one of his own. Whatever kind of gloss he tried to put on his predicament, there was no getting away from it. Here he was, good old Bert Royal, last of that hard-drinking, hell-raising bunch of detectives who called themselves Rivers's Raiders, conspiring with the Deputy's despised rubber heels. That's what brought on the pains. That's what really went against the grain.

'Looks like we struck lucky this time,' Vicky said as she peered intently through the windscreen and watched Bogan disappear into the Trade Winds.

'Looks like what?' Royal came out of his reverie and twisted around to face her. 'So he stopped off at a supermarket. Where's the harm in that?'

Vicky's hand went down to the door handle. 'He's off his beat, he's out of uniform, a pound to a penny he's up to his tricks again.' Her face set. 'And I'm going after him.'

'Hang on a minute.' Royal laid a restraining hand on her arm. 'Maybe he just stopped off for a loaf of bread or something.'

'Oh yeah?' She jutted her jaw and there it was, that stubborn expression on her face, just like her old man. Once more Royal felt the tug of the years. She had her father's look all right, the same cobra stare, ready to exploit any hint of weakness, just like Jack Rivers in his prime. It was uncanny.

'My money says he's on the take—' Vicky released the door catch—'and I'm going to nail him with his hand in the till.'

Those eyes bored defiantly into Royal's face. 'Stay here

if you want, pretend it isn't happening, but you can't stop me going in.'

That puggish tilt of her face that was pure Jack brought it back, the anguish of a memory Bert Royal most wanted to be shot of. The darkness of the office broken only by the yellow cone from a reading lamp and Jack Rivers slumped forward into that pool of dismal light, the glass tumbler dispensed with as he drank whisky straight from the bottle and harangued the rusty iron bar lying on the blotter in front of him. That was how Royal had found him, so deep in his cups that he had lost touch with reality. His own cheeks wet with tears of grief, Royal had hauled his old pal to his feet and had half-carried him out of the headquarters building by a back entrance so that they wouldn't be seen, Jack's head lolling on his shoulder, the bloodshot eyes uncomprehending, the blue-veined nose snuffling against his coat. The legend had drowned in the bottle that night and two weeks later Jack Rivers's heart gave out and an era came to an end. Eager new faces spouting computer jargon were taking over the CID and to save himself from the same fate, Bert Royal, last of the old stagers, asked for a transfer to uniform to work out his final years in the job. Now Jack's face had come back to haunt him.

'Look, Vicky—' he shook his head to break the spell—'be reasonable. You can't just march in there. Bogan's an old hand. Even assuming this is what you think it is, you follow him in there, he'll clock you a mile off and you'll blow the whole thing.'

'Then show me how.' Vicky threw down the gauntlet. 'Show me how you and the great Jack Rivers used to do it back in the good old days, or have you lost your touch?'

Royal let go her arm, the challenge hanging in the air between them. According to standing orders, a minimum of ten detectives was needed to tail a target. The ploy had a fancy name, peripheral pivotal surveillance, a mosaic of shadows acting out an elaborate ballet, but old Jack had always scorned such sophistication. He remembered the time when the two of them had commandeered a painter's van and spent hilarious hours daubing emulsion around a back street hotel as they worked their way to the room where a major villain was holed up. Slipped past the bodyguards and hit him like a ton of bricks. All it took was barefaced cheek.

'Don't push your luck, Inspector,' Royal told her gruffly, getting out of the car. 'Me and your dad could run rings around the pansies we've got in the job these days.' He went to the boot, opened the lid and pulled out the old green Barbour and flat cap he kept for walking the dog, and put them on, transforming himself into a bumpkin up from the country. 'Tell you what. I'll give you a shot at playing detective, Vicky, but that just about uses up your credit with me. You show out in there and I'm pulling rank and kicking you off my sub-division so fast your feet won't touch the ground.'

Vicky came around the car. 'You've got a deal,' she said, smiling, and they began to walk towards the entrance to the Trade Winds, her high heels clicking on the tarmac. As they neared the glass doors she took Royal's arm and gave it a grateful squeeze. 'Come on,' she said, 'let's go shopping.'

The glass doors slid shut behind him and Bogan paused for a moment, taking in the scene, the swirl of shoppers pushing their laden carts, and then, with the old casual swagger in his step, he strolled down the line of checkouts casting his eye over the girls in their green and white striped smocks perched at the tills. Ignoring a sign which said STAFF ONLY—NO ADMITTANCE, he went through a door at the far end of the line and up the stairs to the management quarters on the first floor.

Down a pale green corridor with prints of sailing ships on the walls Bogan found the manager's office, and with his usual disregard for the normal courtesies, walked in without knocking.

A hard-faced woman, ash blonde, with heavy make-up, was behind a tubular metal desk, hammering away at a word-processor, sending lines of text skipping across the grey screen. She looked up and gave the intruder a mascara scowl.

'Hello, gorgeous,' Bogan greeted her breezily as he stepped inside, heading for the inner sanctum, 'we still got a date tonight?'

The glass doors jerked open again as Vicky, pushing a wire shopping trolley ahead of her, crossed the threshold into the background roar of the air-conditioning and the rasp of the checkout printers. Shuffling along beside her, Bert Royal was just in time to catch a glimpse of Bogan disappearing through the staff door. 'Look, there he goes.' Vicky spotted him too and slewed the trolley, catching Royal's shin. He winced at the sharp pain as she let go of the cart and was all for pursuing her quarry, but Royal held her back. 'Don't be daft,' he whispered in her ear, 'you go in there and you're snookered. We're going to have to play this one on a long line.'

'And let him off the hook?' She tried to shake off his hand, but Royal tightened his grip. 'We'll do this my way,' he said, 'or not at all.' He took the handle of the trolley and, towing Vicky behind him, trundled across towards the cover of the first aisle. What did they look like, Royal wondered, noting the barbed glances of the matrons whose progress their spat had impeded: father and daughter, uncle and niece, middle-aged cradle snatcher? He pulled up in the lee of the news-stand, rack upon rack of brightly coloured magazines and periodicals and swung Vicky around, her face close to his. 'Get some groceries in this thing, and make it look good—' he clamped her hand on the trolley—'work your way down to the far end where you can keep an eye on that door and don't move a muscle until I tell you, understood?'

Vicky pouted her frustration, but did as she was told, and Royal, stationed at his vantage-point, took a magazine from the rack at random and began to leaf through the pages, one eye on the staff door, willing Bogan to reappear. A sniff at his elbow startled him. A top-heavy brunette in a padded jacket and tight ski pants was giving him a cold look and Royal's gaze fell to the periodical in his hand. To his dismay he saw he had picked up a lingerie catalogue.

Without so much as a falter in the tattoo she was beating on the keyboard, the mascara queen gave Bogan the freeze through a veil of black widow lashes. 'That'll be the day,' she replied with a laconic arch of a pencilled brow. 'You try that line with all the girls?'

'Only the sexy ones,' Bogan said, moving past her. 'You don't know what you're missing.'

'Oh, I can imagine,' she replied, 'and if you're looking for his nibs, you won't find him in there.'

The inner door stood ajar and through the gap Bogan checked that the office beyond was indeed empty. He turned, a grin on his face. 'Got you alone at last then, eh?' He leaned over the desk. 'Why don't you lock the door and try my special offer?'

Text stuttered monotonously across the screen as she batted him off. 'No, thanks, might spoil my lunch.' She inclined her head. 'You'll find old misery-guts down on the floor, having a nervous breakdown. Been doing his crust all morning. You'd think we'd never done a stock-taking before.'

Unwilling to abandon a challenge, Bogan gave her his big ice-melting smile. 'Sure you won't change your mind? You know what they say, lunch is for wimps.'

Her fingers increased speed. 'Not even if you give triple stamps. If I don't finish this report before he gets back, he'll be like a bear with a sore head for the rest of the day. So do me a favour, sweetie, sling your hook.'

Bogan didn't push it, he simply chalked up a miss. Fancy waking up with that sourpuss on the pillow beside you, he consoled his ego as he retraced his steps back down into the store.

Vicky Rivers dawdled at a freezer cabinet piled high with frozen chickens, her attention distracted by a couple in designer casuals who were surreptitiously grazing the shelves. In the Bake Away they had nibbled chocolate croissants, under the Fresh Produce sign they had sampled the grapes, and now they seemed poised to plunder the sheer cliff of brightly packaged biscuits. With their haughty looks and sly moves she couldn't understand why one of the assistants tending the shelves hadn't spotted such blatant thieving, until it dawned upon her that they were dead-eyed zombies, oblivious of the rugby scrum of humanity jostling around them bent to the serious toil of cramming their trolleys to the limit. Fired up with indignation, she began to manœuvre her own cart, into which she had dumped a dozen or so items for the sake of appearances, to head them off, spoil their little game. Vicky took a quick glance over her shoulder at the staff door she was supposed to be watching and stopped dead in her tracks. The sudden braking caused the trolley to swerve across the aisle and she found the grazers staring at her. Instead of challenging them, she mumbled an apology and brushed by, heading down the canyon of Pasta Products at a fast clip. In that split second the door had opened and Bogan had reappeared.

Alan Potter was in Fresh Produce putting the final flourish to a pyramid of pineapples under a gaudy blow-up of a tropical beach scene. The pinstriped store manager wore his slicked-down hair scraped across his skull from somewhere near his left ear and behind gold-rimmed bifocals his watery eyes looked permanently perplexed. He was bent over, fussing with the display, when Bogan came up behind him and said, 'Those look nice and ripe, Alan, you pick 'em yourself?'

Potter unfolded in a jerky movement, blinking rapidly. 'Jesus, Bogan,' he protested, 'you're going to give me a heart attack, creeping up like that.' He looked at his watch. 'Where the hell have you been? You were supposed to be here an hour ago.'

'Keeping our fair city safe for honest citizens to go about their daily toil, Alan,' Bogan replied. The prissy manager reminded him of Rip-Off Ralph, Iris's supper guest. They both had that sleek, well-fed look about them. His lip curled as he laid on the sarcasm. 'So they can scrape up enough to pay off the credit card the missus brings in here so you can fleece her blind.' He looked around, his expression becoming a smirk. 'Business looks pretty good, so what's the panic?'

Potter grew agitated. 'We had intruders on the roof again last night, bust a skylight this time and damn nearly got in. I called your lot but they didn't want to know and now I've got the regional manager breathing down my neck. The watchman called me out and I dialled 999 and practically got my head bitten off. I report a crime, for God's sake, and nobody turns up. What the hell's going on?'

'Priority policing, Alan,' Bogan explained cheerfully, enjoying the manager's chagrin. 'Like I told you before, it's all the rage these days. We're working on a ten-point code for emergency response and shadows in the night don't even raise an eyebrow.'

'Am I supposed to tell him that? The police don't want to know?'

'Watch my lips,' Bogan told him. 'You want insurance, you've got to pay the premiums, just like BUPA. Tell him you're getting the best security money can buy.'

'Oh yeah? I tell him that and I'll get crucified. I told him I'd sort it out.'

'Take it easy, Alan,' Bogan said. 'You'll burst a blood vessel. Look, the way I see it you've got a choice. Get some fancy firm in and they'll charge you an arm and a leg fitting infra-red sensors all over the place and the maggots'll foam the box, blow the electronics you just paid a fortune for, and clean you out. Or you could do it cut price, get a couple of deadbeats with a mangy Alsatian and see how safe you feel then. See what kind of story you can cook up for your boss when you come in one morning and find you've been done over. Only don't come crying to me because by then you'll be way past the sell-by date. Market forces, Alan. When it comes to security, you can't beat the personal touch.'

'If I had a decent budget I wouldn't have to bother with all this hole-and-corner stuff,' Potter lamented. 'Head office strips me to the bone and then expects me to work miracles.' He sighed. 'Last night was the last straw. So what do I have to do?'

Bert Royal cut through Pickles and Sauces, slipped down Canned Soup alley, and caught up with Vicky Rivers at the Pizza carousel where twenty different toppings were on offer. 'Looks like we're in business,' she told him, inclining her head to where Bogan and the pinstripe were in conversation. Without waiting for an opinion, she led him back down the aisle and pointed out a framed display set into the sea-green wall tiles at the customer service point. 'Recognize anybody?' Vicky asked triumphantly. Royal studied the management team portraits under the Trade Winds logo, the sickly smiles of the general manager, his deputy, the staff manager and the checkout manager beamed back at him.

'That's our man,' she said, pointing to Potter. 'Mr Smarm himself. Now do you believe me?'

Royal took a packet of muesli from a nearby shelf and began to read the contents. 'Still don't prove anything,' he said, head down, avoiding her eyes.

'Bet I could, though, if we sneaked up on 'em.'

Royal dropped the muesli into the wire basket and shrugged deeper into his coat. 'You never let up, do you?'

'Not when I know I'm right.'

Royal glanced over the bobbing, weaving heads to where Bogan and the store manager were still in conversation. If Vicky was right, he didn't have a choice. 'You know what I was just thinking,' he said. 'What if that was me down there, what would you do?'

Her smile was brittle. 'How'd it go—"without fear or favour, affection or ill-will."' She repeated the oath they all took when first they donned the uniform, and Royal felt a chill seep into his bones.

Bogan picked a pineapple from the pyramid and turned it over in his hand. 'I'd say you were ripe, Alan. Last night was just a trial run to test out your defences. Now they know you're wide open, they'll be back.'

'That's all I needed.' Potter's face sagged. 'If that happens, they're going to be sending their hatchet men down from head office to see what's going on and how'm I supposed to tell 'em I'm slipping you a backhander? Are you going to come down here and explain the security system? Not in a million years.'

'You know your trouble, Alan,' Bogan said. 'You've got no imagination. Look on the bright side and I'll take the problem off your hands. Tell you what I'm going to do. Get some quarter-inch steel sheet, the stuff they use in the dockyard down the road, and a couple of guys I happen to know who're handy with a welder. Make some nice strong shutters to lock down over your Mickey Mouse skylights and you can sleep easy in your bed.'

'You think so?' Potter looked more hopeful.

'Guarantee it,' Bogan said. 'The only way they're going to get in then is with acetylene cutters and no self-respecting breaker's going to give himself a hernia lugging the tanks and the torch up on to your roof just so he can lay his hands on a few melons. Do yourself a favour before it hits the fan. Stump up the premium and you're on high risk cover.'

Potter sighed as his hand went into the inside pocket of his jacket and came out with a thick manila envelope. 'I hope you're right,' he said, handing it over. 'They start checking up and my job's on the line.'

'You're in good hands, Alan,' Bogan said, tucking the packet inside his tunic. 'Couple of days and this'll all blow over and you'll wonder what the fuss was about.'

The store manager stared at the picture behind the mountain of pineapples and wished he could transport himself to that tropical beach. Reflected in the chrome of the display stand, he caught sight of a couple of his customers lingering over the fresh fruit, pictured a young woman helping her father with the family shop, losing patience with the old boy in his ratty Barbour and greasy flat cap. As one weight lifted from his shoulders, the roaring, jousting turmoil of front-line commerce dumped another load, which settled even more heavily.

Turning on his heel, Bogan said, 'Cheer up, Alan, business is business, and besides—' he tossed the pineapple which Potter caught clumsily—'the man from Del Monte says yes.'

CHAPTER 10

Jojo walked the last hundred yards down to the Arrow Bridge. Traffic was bottlenecked on the plaza which funnelled four lanes into the toll-booths standing sentinel over the span. Lamps blinked red and green as coins dropped into the palms of the guardians of the bridge.

Stepping out in her trainers and turquoise shell, Jojo headed for the pedestrian walkway along the outer edge of the tarmac deck which bore a steady stream of cars and lorries. She was thinking about Gary and the day he had taken her to see the little terraced house he had renovated in Cromwell Street. The houses had been nothing more than a snaggle-toothed row of Victorian two-up, two-down, back to back slums squatting in the final stages of urban decay, until the developers had snapped them up for a song and had set about transforming the neighbourhood into a desirable mews. Gary escorted her from the pick-up and she let him take her inside, feeling only the cold ice of Michael's betrayal lying in the pit of her stomach. First there was the not unpleasant smell of new wood and fresh paint, then there was the illusion of light and space which he had created within such a meagre structure. He showed her around with animated enthusiasm, taking her hand, touching her and guiding her step on the open staircase. In the bedroom she imagined the neat plastic double glazing draped with Laura Ashley prints, the hardboard floor clad in tufted Wilton, antique brass bedheads gleaming in soft lamplight. He put his arm around her and she didn't resist. Under his clumsy embrace her shoulders began to heave.

'Jojo? Are you all right?' There was concern in his voice, and something else, a tenderness she couldn't cope with. 'You know . . . you must know how I feel about you . . .'

he stammered, but she turned away from him, snuffling.

'Not now, Gary,' she pleaded, 'please, not now.' He gave her his handkerchief, looking miserable and empty as a husk. Jojo drew no joy from his expression of devotion, just found herself pathetically grateful for the close proximity of another warm human being as she clung to him, the sobs racking her body. From that moment on the neat cosy world she had spun around herself began to fall to pieces.

The walkway was protected by a waist-high guard rail and as Jojo passed the toll-booths and walked on to the bridge she saw the man who had spoken to her in the lay-by behind one of the windows. He smiled and waved and she waved back. The first tower was coming up and she craned her neck and shielded her eyes, following it up to the sky where it seemed to pierce the clouds, held back only by the tangle of girders sweeping down from its summit. Her eyes came back to the span vibrating under her feet from the steady rumble of traffic, and she leaned on the rail and looked down to the river four hundred feet below. A coaster the size of a water-beetle was making slow progress against the tide, trapped in the V of its own wake. Jojo put her hands on the iron rail and lifted herself.

'Hey!' the shout came from behind her. Was it Michael, was it Gary calling to her? She didn't look around. 'Hey!' the shout came again, louder, more insistent, but she was concentrating, swinging her legs up between her braced arms and then straightening like a gymnast, gripping the rail with her toes through the thin soles of her kickers, finding her balance as she teetered above the void. 'Hey! What d'you think you're doing? Come off! Come off, for God's sake, or you'll fall!' Out of the corner of her eye she saw the door of a toll-booth fly open and a figure running towards her, arms waving. The words he was shouting seemed out of sync with the movement of his mouth. She almost laughed as everything external geared down into slow motion. She felt no fear at all as her own rhythm raced away and she made the leap for the ladder which went up the outside of the tower, grabbed the rungs and began to climb.

Vicky Rivers was all for grabbing her man there and then but Royal talked her out of it. 'All you've got is circumstantial. Blow the whistle now and he'll laugh in your face.' He shook his head at her impetuosity. 'You've got to build a case so it's watertight, something good and solid you can hit him with. It's called evidence.'

'But you just saw it with your own eyes,' Vicky protested. 'What he put in his pocket.'

Royal said, 'Look, this isn't a penny-ante tea-leaf you're dealing with here. Right now it's your word against his, won't cut much ice on a discipline. Play out the line a little, use your brains.'

Love of God! Royal brought himself up sharp. He was talking about a cop, one of his own, even thinking of him as bent when there could still be an innocent explanation. Beside him, Vicky watched Bogan weaving towards the exit and despite her instincts she knew that the old stager was right. As things stood, she'd never make it stick, not even a dereliction of duty. Go back to the Deputy with nothing but supposition and he'd give her the mackerel eye over his half-moon spectacles and kick her out of the office.

She turned to Royal, the wire trolley between them. 'So what d'you suggest?'

Royal wanted to say, 'Walk away.' Christ alight, he had problems enough without getting tangled up in the interminable ramifications of a discipline. But when he spoke he could hear Jack Rivers expounding his own brand of low cunning. 'You're going after the wrong man.' He inclined his head towards the store manager who was also watching the departing figure. 'Crack the easy nut first.'

Still holding the pineapple, Alan Potter turned back to the display and placed it on top of the pyramid, gazed into the idyllic scene, and daydreamed himself on to the sunkissed beach under that ridiculously perfect palm. Oh boy, he needed a holiday.

'Mr Potter.' The sound of his name made him swing around, the executive smile he had worked so hard to perfect fixed on his pallid face. A couple of customers had come over, lugging their wire trolley, the slightly comical pair he had noticed before, only now something had changed. The old codger had straightened up, looked somehow more sprightly, and the girl was speaking, taking something out of her handbag.

'Yes . . . can I help you?' Potter gave them his attention, and all at once felt a terrible foreboding. Looking grim, the girl showed him a plastic ID with her picture on it. 'We're police officers,' she said.

Feeling pleased with himself, Bogan came out through the automatic glass doors of the Trade Winds and walked back to where he had left the police car. He put a self-congratulatory swagger into his step, for despite his lowly position in the monolithic pyramid of the force he considered himself a more brilliant innovator than the top brass. With only a handful of officers chasing their tails on the million and one pointless errands which bogged down the process of law enforcement, and the city's worthies screaming for their money's worth in terms of police cover, the door was wide open for privatization, and Bogan, having spotted the niche, had no intention of leaving such rich pickings to the private security cowboys. Keeping an eye on the Trade Winds could prove to be a nice touch, and if Alan Potter wanted special attention, then there was no reason why he shouldn't get it, for a price. Bogan the buccaneer, eye to the main chance. He saw Ralph's sweaty face over the candles and thought Iris would be proud of him, smiled to himself as he walked back to the Montego. He could see Nigel Wilcox in there, glued to the radio, raring to go, eager to win his spurs. Had he been like that once? Full of ambition and high moral values? Once upon a time, before his knees creaked and his gut bulged over his belt, had he really rushed home with tales of daring police work? The thought of Iris giving him the shrew treatment extinguished the smile. Didn't the stubborn bitch realize she was the only woman he truly loved? An ache of desperation gnawed at him. There had to be a way he could make her change her mind.

When he reached the Montego he went around to the passenger's side and told Nigel, 'You're driving now, hot-shot. Might as well see how you can handle this heap of junk. Shift over.'

Nigel slid behind the wheel and as Bogan got in beside him asked, 'Any problems in there?'

'Nothing I couldn't handle,' Bogan replied without elaboration. 'You see any desperadoes out here?'

Nigel shook his head. 'Delta Victor were trying to raise us, though.' He nodded towards the radio.

'Oh yeah,' Bogan replied without interest. 'Silly sods think we're waiting on them, they've got another think coming. Let's go.'

Nigel started the engine and did his best to hide his frustration. Twiddling his thumbs in the car park, he had failed to decide whether his mentor's cavalier attitude to the job was the essence of the fabled street cop's intuition, or the manifestation of a work-shy uniform-carrier marking time to the pension. With the radio screaming for them and his own sense of loyalty preventing him from responding, Nigel had turned the question over and over in his mind. Thus far he had been unable to come up with a convincing answer.

He pulled out of the car park on to the street. 'Where to now?'

Bogan pointed through the windscreen towards the superstructure of the Arrow Bridge. 'Go down to the bridge, make a left at the island and head back up town. You like Chinese?'

'We had a couple of students from Hong Kong in my digs. Seemed all right—'

'Chinese nosh, you prat,' Bogan said. 'Sweet and sour, spare ribs, prawn foo yung.'

'Oh, sure.'

Bogan rubbed his hands. 'Meal break coming up,' he said. 'Might drop in at the Slow Boat, get Charlie Chan to knock us up a couple of specials. One thing you've got to remember about the beat, Nige, look after the inner man. Forget that slop they dish up in the canteen. When you ride with me, you eat like a king. OK?'

'I thought we were going in to get the radio fixed?'

'That can wait. Your education comes first.' They were coming up to the bridge approach and Bogan spotted a pair of telephone kiosks on the street corner up ahead. He pointed through the windscreen. 'But seeing as you're so worried, pull over by the TKs there and I'll call in.'

Inside the glass booth Bogan dropped a pound into the slot and tapped out the number on the keypad. When Miss Snooty-Breeches answered he put on an Irish brogue and asked for Mrs Bogan in Accounts. The door-chime 'Greensleeves' played in his ear.

'Hello, Accounts,' he heard Iris say.

'Oh hello, is this Mrs Bogan?' Bogan asked, keeping up the lilt in his voice.

'Yes, speaking.'

'This is Leprechaun Travel calling to tell you you've just won a weekend for two in Paris.'

'A what?'

'Our second honeymoon special, very romantic.'

'You must have the wrong person.'

'Didn't your husband tell you? Maybe he wanted to keep it a secret.'

'Who did you say you are?'

'Leprechaun Travel, we're the little people who make your wish come true,' Bogan said, the accent faltering.

'Like hell,' she said suspiciously. 'It's you again, isn't it?'

'Yeah, it's me,' Bogan confessed. 'If you don't fancy Paris, pick your place, anywhere you like.'

'Bogan, you're impossible.'

She didn't sound too angry and so Bogan said, 'I just wanted to know if you'd changed your mind, about the weekend.'

'I told you, no. No way. I know you, Bogan. I give you an inch, you'll take a mile. We've been through all this before, remember?'

'Iris, for Christ's sake, what've I got to do to stop you giving me a hard time? I just want to see you, that's all, where's the harm?'

'You still don't get it, do you?'

'What's there to get?'

'You and me, it's over. Just stay out of my life.'

'You don't mean that.'

'Every word. Thanks for the blarney, now I'm hanging up.'

'No, wait! When will you talk to me?'

'When you grow up,' Iris said, and she put the phone down.

Bogan felt elated. He had the distinct impression that she was weakening, and if he kept up the pressure, eventually he would wear her down. He pushed the kiosk door open and stepped out on to the pavement in time to see a man running down the road from the direction of the Arrow Bridge waving his arms. He was middle-aged, wearing glasses and he was running full tilt, his arms flailing a frantic semaphore which spelt trouble. Bogan felt the hairs on his neck begin to rise. He walked quickly back to the police car, pulled open the door and said: 'Get out of here.'

But as Bogan jumped in on the passenger's side, Nigel was getting out from behind the wheel, his attention on the running man. Bogan leaned across and tried to grab his arm. 'Get back in and drive, dammit. We've got no business here.'

In desperation, Bogan threw himself into the driving seat fully prepared to do the job himself and leave his green crewmate stranded, but he was too late. The running man was upon them. He doubled over, supporting himself with both hands on the bonnet of the Montego, gasping for breath. Bogan got out again. Nigel was helping the man upright, saying something which Bogan couldn't make out. He went around and pushed his partner aside.

'What's your game?' Bogan growled.

'The bridge!' the man wheezed.

'What?'

'The bridge! The bridge!'

'What about the bloody bridge?' Bogan tried to pull the man off the bonnet of the car but he was a dead weight.

'The woman!'

'What woman?'

'On the bridge!'

'What?'

'I just seen her . . .'

'Hold on a minute . . .'

'. . . on the bridge . . .' The man panted a few words at a time. 'Climbing . . .' He caught his breath '. . . up the bridge, the tower.' He grabbed the lapel of Bogan's tunic. 'You've got to help her!'

'Help who?' Bogan demanded. He saw Nigel's face, eager with anticipation. 'He's serious,' Nigel said. 'We'd better take a look.'

Bogan turned away. 'Love of Christ,' he moaned in a low voice, 'don't let this happen to me.' Nigel hustled the man in the back of the police car. When he had calmed down he told them his name was Peter Fry and he was a toll attendant at the Arrow Bridge. 'I didn't believe my eyes,' he said. 'I mean, I saw her, the woman, I saw her walking on to the bridge, just walking like normal. I didn't think anything of it, you know? Next time I look, she's up on the rail. I couldn't believe what I was seeing. Then, cool as you like, she jumps on to the ladder, and she's going up the tower.'

'You sure?' Bogan asked. 'Couldn't have been a trick of the light or something?'

'I tell you she went up the ladder like a monkey on a stick. I never saw anything like it in my life. I mean, this was your everyday normal sort of lady, not the weirdos we get on the bridge.' He shook his head in disbelief. 'She seemed so nice and ordinary, I wouldn't have believed in a million years she'd've pulled a stunt like that. She's got to be out of her mind.'

Nigel started the car and began to drive towards the bridge. Over his shoulder he said, 'How'd you know she was so ordinary? Did you see her before?'

'That's right,' Fry said. 'He's right,' he said to Bogan, 'I saw her in the lay-by up the top when I was coming to work.'

'Did she have a banner or anything?' Bogan asked.

'A what? No, no, I don't think so. She was just, you know, sort of admiring the view.'

'You spoke to her?' Nigel said.

'Sure, I said good-morning.'

'You're a friendly sort of fellow, eh, Peter?' Bogan said.

'I just passed the time of day,' Fry said. 'Look, Officer, I can spot a nutter a mile off, you don't have to tell me how to spot a nutter, I've had plenty of practice. She wasn't a nutter.'

'So this woman you said good morning to,' Bogan said. 'Just being friendly. You fancy her or something?'

'Hey, what is this?' Fry demanded.

'Easy, Peter,' Bogan said. 'We're just trying to work out what's going on here, that's all. You come charging up the street, all lathered up, telling us there's some loony on the bridge, we just want to get the total picture.'

'I just said hello, that's all, she wasn't a loony.'

'When you said hello, you're sure you didn't see she had a streamer, Save the Whales, something like that, this lady-friend of yours.'

'Look, I told you, she didn't have anything like that. I never set eyes on her before this morning, but you want to know what she was like?'

'Yeah, you told us,' Bogan said, 'She was sort of . . .'

'Ordinary,' Fry said. 'In one of those shell suit things, turquoise, smart-looking lady, but casual, you know?'

Nigel pulled on to the bridge approach. The tolls had shut down, the signals showing four reds, and traffic was backing up. Drivers were getting out of cars and lorries and a crowd was beginning to gather as the word spread. There was a jumper on the bridge! Necks craned, hands shielded eyes scanning the superstructure. When he could move no further forward because of the traffic snarl Nigel pulled in to the side and stopped the Incident Car, goggling through the windscreen at the sea of faces which turned expectantly at the arrival of the new players. The free show was about to begin.

'Let's see what we've got here.' Bogan ground his teeth. 'Pound to a penny it's some kind of stunt.'

Nigel said, 'Didn't we ought to call Delta Victor?'

'Not till we have to,' Bogan said. 'Whistle up the cavalry for some silly bitch on an ego trip, we'd never hear the last of it.' He got out of the car, a sinking feeling tugging at his bowels. 'We'll take a squint, check it out first.' He scowled at the growing band of spectators. 'Looks like we've got the world and his wife for company.' He turned to Fry. 'That the tower?'

Fry said, 'That's it. There's a ladder goes up the side, for the maintenance crew.'

'You'd better come with us,' Bogan said. 'It's your

bridge, you can show us the ropes, and don't even think about sloping off. When this is over I'm going to cop a statement off you.'

They got out of the car and the crowd parted to let them through, like gladiators stepping into the forum. Fry pointed at the top of the tower, vindication in his voice. 'There! What'd I tell you, there she is.'

Bogan shaded his eyes with his hand and stared upwards along the line of Fry's outstretched arm. He followed the ladder up to the tangle of girders near the top of the tower from which the main cables swept away in their graceful arc. He could make out the woman, minute against the sky, leaving the catwalk and climbing out on to the high steel.

'I told you,' Fry exclaimed. 'Didn't I tell you? There she is, you believe me now?'

Bogan swore viciously. This was the very worst kind of trouble to get into, like walking around in a minefield, waiting for something to blow up in your face. Staring at the figure perched precariously up there on the bridge, the spectators watching with bated breath, waiting for him to start the pantomime, Bogan knew the risks, he'd been there before, but when he turned to Nigel he saw spaniel eyes and irrational anger boiled up inside him. The carrot-top hadn't a clue, that was obvious, but Bogan didn't have time to make allowances, and he didn't see the green kid any more, just the uniform. The hell with it, he told himself, he wasn't going to risk his hide just for some show-off on the lousy bridge. It was self-preservation time.

Bogan drew Nigel over to the rail at the base of the tower. 'We've got to wrap this up fast,' he began.

Nigel nodded. 'What's the drill, Ted?' he asked innocently using Bogan's Christian name for the first time.

Bogan said, 'Probably it's just a stunt, but we can't take a chance. You're going to have to go up and get the silly cow to come down before this turns into a circus.'

Nigel blinked. He had expected something else, some

well-oiled emergency plan to swing into operation. Special equipment, trained professionals moving sure-footed to the rescue. He hadn't imagined . . .

'Look, Nige,' Bogan pressed on, 'I'd do it myself, only . . .'

'Can't we raise somebody?' Nigel stammered, knowing full well that he would be gripped by vertigo and paralysed with fear the moment he so much as contemplated climbing up there.

'Nigel,' Bogan said, 'you think I want to send you up there if there was some way I could avoid it? Only we're stuck with it, there's people watching.' He looked around, 'Bloody exhibitionist, some stupid bitch!'

Bogan's fear was infectious and Nigel picked up the scent and began to sweat cold. 'I don't know if I can do it, Ted.'

'Come on,' Bogan reassured him. 'Just take it nice and easy, you'll be all right. I'll give you a boost up and you're on the ladder. Be a cinch.'

'Ted, I don't think . . .'

'I'll call it in and get us some back-up, no sweat.'

'Ted . . .'

'Nige, listen to me, I'm fat and I'm forty and I get nose-bleeds on a step ladder . . .'

'. . . I still don't think . . .'

'You've got no choice.' Bogan's patience snapped and the musk of his own fright thickened the air. 'This is what it's all about.'

Bent forward, hands cupped, he told Nigel to put his foot in the stirrup so that he could boost him on to the scaling ladder. There was betrayal in the spaniel eyes and he couldn't look into them. A collective sigh escaped from the crowd.

'Fuck it, Nigel,' Bogan resorted to the only accusation he could muster. 'You wanted to be a fucking copper.'

CHAPTER 11

Hanging out over the void which went clear down to the pewter-grey river four hundred feet below, Nigel clung to the spindly iron ladder and felt only the tingling numbness of fear draining his strength away. Bogan's words sang inside his head like the twang of a taut wire and he willed himself to subdue the beguiling voice of vertigo which whispered to him to throw himself into the arms of the abyss. Clenching his teeth until his jaw ached, Nigel flattened himself against the ladder, nervously testing the rungs. After what seemed like an eternity he succeeded in shouting down the competing voices. Gingerly he began to climb.

The silence was absolute as he inched his way up the tower which reared above him and he began to feel terrible pangs of loneliness as he gulped air through his mouth and tried to feed oxygen to his galloping heart. He knew, whatever else happened, he must not allow himself to hyperventilate and lose control of his bodily functions. Bogan was right, he was a police officer and certain attributes of courage and tenacity were rightfully expected of him. He knew that the eyes of the crowd on the bridge were following his every move and with pathetic bravado he vowed not to let his partner down. Pride spurred him on, but he was running on empty.

Nigel climbed cautiously, gripping each rung so tightly that his knuckles hurt, working his way upwards, hand over hand, never daring to look down. It became curiously easy, using the ladders and the catwalks provided for maintenance and when he reached the buttress of girders supporting the main cable from which the bridge was suspended, he was surprised by its size. It was like a great tree-trunk dipping away in a graceful arc. From his perch in the nest of girders he could make out the figure of the woman. She had gone some distance down the cable and had swung herself below it to sit on a cross spar with her legs dangling over the void. He contemplated calling out to her from the comparative safety of the tower, but decided that might just spook her into jumping. A solid wedge of fear thrust itself into Nigel's throat and threatened to choke him, but with a supreme effort of will he managed to persuade his limbs to respond and began to crawl down the cable, wriggling forward, arms and legs wrapped around its steel girth. He had not gone far before he was gripped by a new, sickening terror. It wasn't a trick of his imagination. The cable was moving!

Nigel clung on desperately, his face pressed against the cold rough metal as a new wave of fear assaulted his body. The superstructure of the bridge was not rigid as he had imagined it to be, it swayed, giving and taking within the tolerances of its design. Clinging to this undulating steel snake five hundred feet above the water, Nigel fought back wave after wave of nausea as he forced himself onwards.

Out of nowhere a voice drifted up to him. 'Come any closer and you're going to be the only one up here.'

When it became obvious he had no alternative Bogan went back to the police car and called in. He knew as soon as Delta Victor logged an on-going incident on the Arrow Bridge into Command and Control the division would go into orbit. In no time at all the bridge would be crawling with tactical teams, negotiators and half the brass from headquarters would be sticking their oar in. But he could see no way around it, even though he knew that first on the scene would be Sergeant Davies looking for an opportunity to rub his nose in it. Not that Bogan doubted his own ability to talk himself out of a tight spot, but he cursed his misfortune that he should find himself on the rack for the sake of a screw-loose jumper.

As luck would have it, Davies was in the control room and took over from the dispatcher.

'Bogan? Where the hell have you been?'

'Radio's playing up, Sarge,' Bogan said into the radio. 'I was coming back in at meal break to get it fixed when we got this shout.'

'Sounds OK to me.'

'It's definitely on the blink, transmission's breaking up in town so I took a run out here, see if it improved. You're right, it is much better.'

'I told you to stay away from that bloody bridge.'

'Oh, just for a radio test, Sarge, that was all, then this bloke flagged us down, said there was a nutter on the bridge.'

'Congratulations,' Davies sighed. 'You just won an award for fiction. I never heard so much eyewash.'

'Uh-huh, the jumper's up there all right.' Bogan sidestepped the barbed response. 'Wilcox has gone after her, like a ferret up a drainpipe.'

He heard Davies groan. 'Don't do anything. If you know what's good for you, don't even move a muscle. Just contain the scene, Bogan, can you manage that?'

'I dunno, traffic's backing up something awful. We need some of the traffic boys pronto, start clearing this mess.'

'Just sit tight, we're going to go by the book on this one, you got that, Bogan? By the book.'

'Do I take it you're coming out, Sarge?' Bogan asked guilelessly.

'Damn right I am,' Davies snapped back. 'I'm first in line to kick your sorry backside from here to breakfast-time. Delta Victor out.'

Bogan threw the handset across the seat, turned around and found Peter Fry, the toll attendant, watching him.

'What are you looking at?' Bogan demanded.

'You told me to stay with you,' Fry said. 'But I tell you

what. I don't fancy your mate's chances up there, not by himself. Are they sending help?'

'Yeah,' Bogan said. 'They're sending help all right.'

'Because that old bridge can be a bitch if the mood takes her,' Fry said. 'She bucked a couple of riggers off there when they were putting her up.'

'Now you tell me,' Bogan said. 'It's my arse in a sling, and now you're telling me the bridge isn't safe. Where's the supervisor?'

'I called the office,' Fry said. 'He's coming in with the maintenance foreman, Jack Jarvis, he knows every rivet on that baby. You said something about a statement.'

'That can wait,' Bogan said. 'I'm more interested in this bird you took a fancy to. You give her the chat and next thing we know she's shinning up the bridge. You want to tell me about that?'

Behind the smudged lenses of the spectacles watery eyes looked pained. 'I told you, it wasn't like that. It wasn't her caught my eye, it was the car.'

'The car? What car?'

'Her car, the big cat, a real beauty . . .'

At the Trade Winds, Vicky said, 'I'm Inspector Rivers and this is Superintendent Royal,' caught the flash of panic crossing the store manager's face as she showed him her warrant card, and added softly, 'Can we go somewhere a little more private?'

Potter led them up to his office and told his hatchet-faced secretary to take an early lunch. Without looking up from her word-processor, she said she hadn't finished the report he had asked for. He told her to forget the report and go to lunch.

In his room, Potter scurried for the safety of his desk, anxious to put the slab of mahogany between himself and his unwanted guests. 'What's this all about?' he asked defensively.

'We think you know, Mr Potter.' Royal took the lead. 'Your little chat with Constable Bogan down there.'

'He solicited a pecuniary advantage from you, didn't he?' Vicky said.

'A what?'

'Payment for services,' Royal translated.

'Or to put it more bluntly, a bribe,' Vicky said.

Potter's eyes swivelled from one to the other. 'I don't know what you're talking about.' A nervous tic jumped down the side of his face.

'Oh yes you do,' Vicky said. She tapped her handbag. 'We've got it all on tape, every word.'

Royal shot her a glance. That was the kind of stunt her old man would have pulled. He turned back to Potter and saw that the barb had achieved the desired effect. The store manager deflated like a pricked balloon, his head sinking between his shoulders, the words gushing out of him in a resentful whine. 'What've I got to do to get through to you people? I'm trying to run a business here, and what'm I getting? Ripped off left, right and centre. Merchandise walking out of this place like there was no tomorrow, staff rooking me blind and tearaways trying to break in the minute my back's turned. What do you lot care? Call the police, you don't want to know. So what'm I supposed to do? Grin and bear it, wait until the shelves are stripped bare, turn out the lights and give up?' Impotent anger flushed his face. 'I'm a businessman. Someone comes along and offers me a deal which looks like it can solve my problem, I'm going to grab it with both hands, so don't come any of this high and mighty pecuniary advantage stuff with me—' He stabbed his chest with a forefinger. 'I pay your wages, I've got to make a living, and I know my rights.'

'Hey, hey, calm down, Mr Potter,' Royal said. 'We're not getting at you, we want your cooperation, that's all.'

'You see—' Vicky conjured a smile—'it's a discipline investigation. It's Bogan we're after.'

'So why don't we try again,' Royal suggested mildly, 'only nice and friendly this time and see if it isn't in your best interests to help us out.'

Potter shook his head. 'I don't believe this. You're after Bogan? We've got crime tearing this town apart, and you're putting the boot into one of your own? What is this, a sick joke?'

'Oh, we're not joking, Mr Potter,' Vicky said. 'One of 'em gets away with it, pretty soon they'll all be at it, and where would we be then?'

'No worse than we are now,' Potter said, 'that's for sure.'

'We don't want to cause you any trouble if we don't have to,' Royal said, still playing along. 'We could probably make a criminal case against you, but we don't want to do that. Help us out and we'll wash our own linen.'

'Internal discipline,' Vicky said.

'So how about it?' Royal made the offer.

Potter read their faces, looking for a sign. They were deadpan. His head continued to wag in disbelief, but he could see they were serious. 'OK,' he sighed, 'what do I have to do?'

Royal was about to lay it out for him when the bleeper on his belt suddenly shrieked. In the same instant the pager in Vicky's handbag went off. Potter flinched as Royal cut off the noise, lunged across the desk for the phone and called the station. Vicky had her bag open on her lap, fumbling in the clutter. She found her bleeper and switched it off, looked up as Royal put the phone down.

'Trouble,' Royal told her ominously. 'Come on, we've got to go.' He jerked a thumb. 'Right now.'

'But . . . but we can't . . . not now.' Vicky's composure was slipping while across the desk Potter just looked dazed.

'Forget it,' Royal snapped, and then to Potter: 'This is your lucky day, my friend. Saved by the bell.'

Vicky exclaimed, 'Hey, just wait a minute.'

'Out.' Royal made it an order, hustling her through the door.

He marched her down the corridor, still complaining, her cheeks burning from the injustice of yanking her out when she had a star witness eating out of the palm of her hand.

'This isn't fair,' Vicky protested. 'I had him right there.' She clenched a fist. 'I'll never get a better chance to—'

'Crucify a brother officer?' Royal let his disgust show. 'You might as well say it, Vicky. Bogan's head on a plate? I'll tell you something for nothing: if your old man could see you now, he'd be spinning in his grave.'

'*Quis custodes*,' Vicky replied hotly. 'Somebody's got to do the dirty work, and I'm going to be the best.' Her cheeks flushed in anger. 'Men—' she spat the word like an oath —'you're all the same, stick together come what may. I thought you were different, Uncle Bert.'

Royal, moving her along, his hand in the small of her back, was suddenly sickened by her zeal to turn over the stones. He couldn't conceal his contempt any longer. 'You think that's police work, Vicky, busting cops? If you're in such an all-fired hurry to make a name for yourself, young lady, now's your chance, you're tactics trained.' She stared at him, her cheeks aglow with pent-up rage and Royal was tempted to let her have it, right there and then. Poor little Vicky Rivers determined to emulate her illustrious old man. Throw it in her face, the guilty secret he and Jack had shared all those years. Show her once and for all that the myth of the great detective was fatally flawed. Instead he ground out the words like broken glass, 'Let's see how you shape up on a really tough one. Bogan's got a jumper on the Arrow Bridge.'

'Let's get this straight. You're telling me the nutter on the bridge was in a car?' Bogan put the question to Peter Fry, trying to make some sense out of the crazy scene on the bridge.

'Well, not in it exactly. Standing by it, up in the lay-by. It was the car, you see, we got talking about the car.'

'Why didn't you tell me this before?'

Fry's pallid face went blank. 'You didn't ask me,' he said.

'Well, I'm asking you now,' Bogan said, a harsh edge of irritation creeping into his voice. 'Tell me about this motor of hers.'

'Prettiest thing you ever saw,' Fry said. 'V12 XJS, low and sleek, power hood, kick down and you get nought to sixty in eight seconds. Hit a hundred and forty easy, even with the old three-speed automatic.'

'She'd got a sports Jag?'

'What else d'you think I just described? Nothing else in the world can hold a candle to the big cat.'

Bogan bundled Fry into the police car. 'Show me,' he said, telling himself that if he had the jumper's car he could run a check on it and at least have something up his sleeve to head off dancing Davies. He drove up the loop against the jammed traffic and swung the Montego into the parking bay. Fry got out and looked around. A puzzled expression formed on his face. The space where the Jaguar had stood was empty.

'She was right here,' he said, standing at the spot and glancing around him as though he expected the big cat to materialize. 'Only now she's gone.'

'Don't suppose you got the number?' Bogan inquired sourly.

Fry shook his head.

'Describe it to me.'

'I told you. She was the big V12 convertible.' He peered at the bare strip of tarmac visualizing the car, 'Long, low profile with the power bulge on the bonnet and the wood and leather cockpit—'

Bogan cut him off. 'If I want the works spec I can go to the showroom, so you can cut out the drooling. What colour was it?'

'Yellow,' Fry recalled instantly. 'Yellow with a white hood. I remember that easy because that surprised me, the colour combination. I never saw a Jag that colour before, must've been a special paint job. I had that kind of money, I'd go for BRG and wires, classy, not something looked like a banana.'

Bogan's eyes narrowed. Yellow XJS with a white rag top? His memory clicked back frame by frame until he had the picture. He glanced at the registration number scrawled on the back of his hand and began to wonder just what the hell was going on.

CHAPTER 12

The yellow Jaguar, white hood up, came out of the Mermaid underpass nudging the legal limit and joined the traffic streaming out of town on the orbital dual carriageway.

Twenty minutes later, indicating left, the XJS took the exit ramp signed Luxton and cruised into the stockbroker belt.

'I still dunno why we didn't do the one in town,' Phil said.

'Because this is better,' Woody said, driving one-handed, the loaded shotgun on the seat beside him. The double barrels were sawn off so short that the crimped ends of the fat 00 Buck cartridges were clearly visible. 'Look around. It's all Jags, Mercs and Porsches around here. We pull up outside the place, nobody's going to bat an eyelid.'

'It's an awful long way to get back,' Phil said, 'where we left the motor.'

'Not in this it isn't,' Woody said. 'We'll be out of here like smoke. Besides, we're going to hit the fat ponces where it hurts most, in the wallet.'

'We could've done that in town.'

'Use your head, dummy. Mr Ponce breezes off to the office, what's Mrs Ponce going to do with her day? Go shopping. And what's she going to need to go shopping? Loadsamoney. So what's the one thing the shylock's going to have on tap? Bags of folding stuff.'

'Not out here,' Phil said. 'It's all credit cards out here.'

'Posers use credit cards,' Woody said. 'The ponces who live around here have bitched and screamed and clawed their way up on the long firms and any other fiddle they could turn their hands to, so they don't trust the plastic, got to be cash on the nail. What d'you think I was doing on the crummy bin round out here, getting fresh air and a suntan? Grow up, Phil.'

The girl in the back seat leaned forward, put her arms around the passenger's seat and nibbled Phil's ear. 'Grow up, Phil,' she mimicked.

The Jaguar cruised down the tree-lined boulevards from which gravel drives stretched back to the ranch bungalows, architect-designed split-levels and mock-Tudor mansions hidden from view behind sculptured shrubbery. A line of shops set back from the road blended tastefully into the landscape. A delicatessen, a fashion boutique called Maison Marcel, a Cornucopia mini store and a trendy hair stylist. The centrepiece was a pink-marble-fronted branch of the Countyset Building Society. Woody double parked alongside a Volvo Estate and, leaving the engine running, motioned Phil to slide over as he opened the door and got out carrying the stubby shotgun close to his body.

He walked quickly around the back of the Jaguar, crossed the pavement and went into the Countyset. As he pushed open the swing door he saw two customers, both women, at the counter. There were six cashiers' positions, four of them manned, three women, one man. In the open plan office behind the counter several clerks were seated at computer terminals. There were no bandit screens above the counter, but the carpet in the customers' area was a nice deep pile dove grey which complemented a selection of chrome and leather easy chairs. Woody took this in at a glance as he strode through the door and his gaze settled on the security camera mounted high on the wall looking down the row of cashiers' positions. He swung the shotgun up from his side and pulled both triggers simultaneously. In the confined space the explosion was deafening. The tableau froze as the blast shattered the video camera and ripped a chunk of plaster from the wall. In the stunned aftermath Woody snapped open the breech, ejected the cartridge cases, put his left hand into this pocket, took out two fresh shells and reloaded. Plaster dust swirled as the scene unfroze and they dived for cover, all except the girl at the first position.

Woody grabbed her by the hair and held the shotgun up to her face. He was smiling. 'If it wouldn't be too much trouble, Miss Jenkins—' he read her name plate—'I'd like to make a cash withdrawal.' He released his grip on her hair and took a black plastic sack from his pocket and handed it to her. 'Fill that from all the tills, just the notes. Do it in fifteen seconds, or I'll blow your fucking head off.' Petrified, the girl began to scrabble at her own cash drawer, stuffing handfuls of notes into the sack. Woody turned the shotgun on the others who were watching him with rabbit eyes. 'Stay absolutely still,' he told them reassuringly, 'I'm not going to hurt anybody I don't have to. But if I have to I'll kill you.' He began to count: One, two, three . . . On the count of twelve, the girl scooped money from the last till and scrambled back down the counter. She handed the sack to Woody.

'The People's Revolutionary Party thanks you, Miss Jenkins.' He bowed. 'It's been a pleasure doing business with you.'

Woody backed to the door. The two women crouched on his side of the counter stared at him, eyes popping from ashen faces. 'Good morning, ladies,' he said, raised a clenched fist in a power salute, turned on his heel, pushed through the door which swung closed behind him as he sprinted to the Jaguar and jumped in. Phil floored the pedal and the big cat took off, laying rubber. Woody tossed the sack to the girl in the back seat. Banknotes fluttered around inside the car as he threw his head back against the restraint and began to laugh.

*

'See what twenty years in the job did for you, Bogan?' Davies said. 'Addled whatever you've got for a brain. Why didn't you call for back-up?'

'What back-up, Sarge?' Bogan said. 'You said it yourself. We're down to the bone on this shift. What back-up you talking about, the Noddy car and the Terrible Twins?'

From where they were standing on the bridge approach Bogan gestured towards a couple of PCs who had slewed their Metro panda across the road and were ineffectually trying to untangle the traffic. 'If the good people of this town knew we've got nothing better than that on the streets, there'd be hell to pay.'

Davies gave Bogan a warning look. 'You know what I'm talking about. Division and HQ. The Super's on his way and he's going to want answers to a few tough questions, like why the hell you let young Wilcox go up there.'

'Oh, I thought you'd want to put the brass in the picture. Chain of command, Sarge, you're the supervisor.'

'And you're the chancer, Bogan. You go swanning off your beat trying to kid me your radio's up the creek. Now you're quoting standing orders. You know what I ought to do? I ought to suspend you right now.'

Bogan smiled. 'Then you'd have nobody left and the gaffers'd start wondering about this hotshot sergeant who gave all his troops white forms just to prove who was the boss. Not many brownie points in that.'

A haunted look appeared in Davies's eyes. Bogan was right. Whatever happened, all the three stripes on his arm qualified him for was to carry the can. 'OK, OK, but for God's sake, you didn't have to send the kid up there.'

'I didn't send him up,' Bogan protested. 'He volunteered. Spouting off about his duty to save life and preserve the peace.' Bogan shrugged. 'You know what these graduates are like, Sarge, keen as mustard. When it comes down to it, they're not going to take much notice of an old sweat like me.'

'Think you're smart, don't you, Bogan.' Davies squinted into his face. 'Got an answer for everything. Well, I've got my eye on you, mister, so you'd better watch your step.'

'Oh, I'm quaking in my boots, Sarge,' Bogan smirked. 'While we're at it, anything else you want to get off your chest?'

'I don't have time to play games with you, Bogan,' Davies said. 'Just fill me in on what's been going on here before the circus arrives. For starters, who's the woman up there?'

Bogan shrugged. 'Search me,' he said. 'Probably just another crank wants to get on the TV. Looks like her wish is going to come true.' He pointed to a Transit van emblazoned with the *Eyewitness News* logo which was threading its way through the stalled traffic, headlights blazing.

'Sweet Jesus,' Davies groaned as he turned to watch the van approach. 'That's all we needed.'

Bogan was anxious to escape from the Sergeant's clutches just long enough to check out the coincidence of the yellow Jaguar. His streetwise intuition told him the number scribbled on the back of his hand would give him the edge and he had no intention of sharing his hunch with the dapper dancer.

'Why don't you give the graduate a shout on the bat-phone?' Bogan suggested. 'What with his fancy degree and his smooth line in chat, I'll bet he's got her life story out of her by now.'

Davies leaned out over the guard rail and peered upwards, shading his eyes with one hand, trying to get a clear sight of his man, but the ironwork of the bridge obscured his view. Suddenly his flesh began to creep as he realized time was running out. Somewhere in the distance he could hear the sound of approaching sirens.

'Hey you! You hear me! I'm warning you, come any closer and you're going to be the only one up here. I mean it.' The warning which floated up rang with an ethereal quality, like the high notes of a choir, and the stultifying terror which engulfed him as he embraced the cable in a desperate bear hug robbed him of the ability to grasp the meaning of the words. All that his tortured senses screamed was that there was another member of his own species close by and, instinctive as an ape in the tree-tops, he locked on to the voice and in one desperate lunge swung himself on to the girder suspended in space below the cable.

Nigel could see the woman close by, the pale oval of her face turned towards him. He began to crawl, not daring to look down, his eyes on her face, knowing that one blink, one split-second lapse of concentration, and he would be finished, succumbing to the blessed relief of his death fall to the river far below. 'Don't worry . . . don't worry . . .' he heard himself stammer as he scuttled along the strip of metal and almost fell into her arms. 'I've . . . I've come to help.' The words sounded so stupid, but the bile was thickening in his throat and he knew he was going to be sick. 'Jesus, I'm . . . I'm sorry . . .' he croaked, bitterly ashamed at his own weakness as he managed to remove his cap and threw up into it, retching uncontrollably.

'Oh boy,' Jojo relented, grabbing hold of him. 'Young Sir Galahad puking all over me. Here, give me that.' She took the cap from his trembling hand and hung it from a bolt head by its strap.

'I'm sorry,' Nigel gasped in relief as the heaving subsided. 'I thought I could do it, but I can't . . . you know? I can't cope with it, the height. I can't stand it.'

'You look like death.' Jojo peered at him, close up.

'I feel like it.'

'So what're you doing up here?'

'Police,' Nigel stammered. 'To help you . . .'

'My God.' Jojo almost laughed. 'That's what you get when you ask a stupid question.' She regarded him for a few seconds longer and then shifted her perch on to a spar where two girders crossed. 'Come over here,' she told him, 'it's safer. Believe me, you look awful.'

Nigel was frozen to the spot. 'I'm sorry . . . I can't move,' he gasped.

'Sure you can . . . Here, trust me, I'll help you.'

She took his hands and guided him on to the crow's nest of the steel cross-section. 'That's better, OK?'

Nigel nodded. The talons of fright still had him in a powerful grip and he couldn't trust himself to speak.

'Just try to relax,' Jojo told him. 'Listen, have you got a cigarette?'

'I . . . I'm sorry . . . I don't smoke,' Nigel managed through chattering teeth.

'Boy, you're a lot of fun, aren't you?' This time she did laugh. 'And I just finished the packet too.'

'I'm sorry.'

'Will you stop saying you're sorry?'

'I'm sorry.'

'Oh Christ, where did they get you from? How old are you anyway?'

'Twenty-two,' Nigel admitted.

'Beautiful,' Jojo said. 'That's all I needed, a junior hero.'

'I just want to help you.' Nigel tried hard but couldn't control the quavering of his voice.

'You want to help me?' Jojo actually laughed this time. 'You're sick, you're terrified, your teeth are chattering, you look like death warmed up and you want to help me? That's rich.'

'You don't understand,' Nigel blurted. 'I have to . . . I took an oath . . . my job.'

'Look,' Jojo said, 'if it'll make you feel any better, we all get one life and the only real choice we get is how we bow out when we can't stand looking at ourselves in the mirror any more. So I came up here to do the one decent thing left, jump off the lousy bridge, and even that gets fouled up, you know? I get landed with you.'

The thread of willpower which Nigel had been able to preserve from his blind fear was wearing thin. His vision had begun to blur and he had lost control of his bowels which appalled him. 'I think . . .' A warm drowsiness washed over him and his self-esteem collapsed. The death plunge beckoned seductively and he imagined the sniggers in the canteen: Stupid dipstick fell off the bridge, what d'you expect from a graduate! Quietly he began to sob. 'I'm sorry . . . I think I'm going to pass out.'

'Oh no you don't,' Jojo told him fiercely. She put her arms around him and drew him close, cradling his head so that he could feel the warmth of her body through the thin shell suit. 'This is my party, nobody's leaving without my permission. You got that?'

An inquisitive seagull made a long swooping pass, diving close to the two figures huddled together high on the latticework superstructure of the Arrow Bridge.

Nigel burrowed between the woman's breasts as she stroked his hair. He had this picture of himself. In the casket at his own funeral, looking down on himself, his astral body soaring like the seagull. The pallbearers in their best uniforms with white gloves. Bogan was one of them, his face expressionless. The aching certainty that he would not get off the bridge alive seeped through him and as he clung to the woman, one question assumed overwhelming importance. 'Can I ask you a question?' he murmured, his face pressed against the turquoise cotton.

'Be my guest,' Jojo replied.

'What's your name?'

CHAPTER 13

'What's his name?' Dave Harris asked, leaning against the wall as Bogan kept his thumb on the doorbell and listened to the echo of the chimes somewhere inside the flat.

'Michael Mitchell,' Bogan said. 'Set up as a diving instructor when he came out of the Andrew, fleecing the tourists.'

'Must be making a good living,' Harris said looking around. 'Place like this must cost a bomb. We're in the wrong line of work, pal.'

Bogan kept his thumb on the button. He'd met up with Harris outside Bosun's Reach, the crescent-shaped block of luxury flats which had popped out of the computer when Bogan ran a PNC check on the registration number scribbled on the back of his hand. The car was registered to a Michael Anthony Mitchell, and this was his address. Before Harris arrived, Bogan had made some cursory door-to-door and had discovered from neighbours that Mitchell lived with a woman who matched the description of the jumper. The connection intrigued him, but before he could pursue his hunch any further Harris had put in an appearance, and he had no intention of sharing his newfound knowledge with this popinjay of a crime squad detective-constable in his silk Valentino jacket and power tie.

'What'd you do to Davies anyway?' Harris folded his arms. 'Stick a nettle up his bum or something? He was practically melting the phone when he called the nick.'

'Davies is a jerk,' Bogan growled. 'Grade A.'

'He don't go much on you either, pal,' Harris said. 'I told him I was out the door on this armed robbery just went off over in Luxton, and he started screaming and pulling rank, told me to get over here and keep an eye on you or I'd be back in a tall hat.' Harris shrugged. 'I mean, it's all the same to me, only I got the distinct impression you're not flavour of the month.'

'I told you,' Bogan said, listening to the chimes, 'Davies is a prat. Don't worry about me, I can take care of myself.'

'Oh, sure,' Harris said. 'Only I've got to watch you like a hawk, make sure you don't pull any strokes. That's what the man said.' Harris chuckled. 'I'm your minder.'

'Don't push your luck,' Bogan said. 'I eat jumped-up sergeants like Davies for breakfast. He don't bother me.'

Harris gave him a toothy grin. 'You putting your papers in, pal, because the only time I heard fighting talk like that before was when the old pension was coming up like an express train. Me, I've got a lot more time to put in on this job, and I don't intend to blot my copybook just because some bolshie PC's having the bags on with his sergeant. So let's get it clear from the off, all right? Don't go giving me any grief.'

'I wouldn't dream of it,' Bogan said, 'ambitious young D like you, Dave. Stick with me, and if it all pans out like I think it will, you'll be in for a commendation.'

'Not the way I see it,' Harris said. 'There would've been more glory in the blagging. Little fucker walks into the Countyset blasting away with a sawn-off and gets six grand for his trouble. Cocky kid thought he'd shot out the security camera, only it was a dummy. They got his ugly mug on a Polaroid, so his collar's as good as felt. Lots of kudos out there, pal, Luxton's all leafy glades, bookies and share sharks eager to show their gratitude. Got style, though, I'll give 'em that. You know what the toe-rags used for a get-away car? Nicked a Jag, yellow XJS convertible.'

Bogan took his thumb off the doorbell and looked at Harris. The yellow Jag was popping up all over the place.

Harris pushed himself off the wall and nodded towards the door. 'Ah, I wondered when you were going to get the message. There's nobody home.'

In frustration Bogan gave the door a perfunctory kick. 'I'm going to boot it in,' he said.

'Not unless you've got a warrant you're not,' Harris told him. 'This isn't some CRO you're taking liberties with. You do that, we'd have his brief down on us like a ton of bricks, suing the chief for unlawful entry. I can see it now.'

Bogan sniffed the air. 'Can't you smell gas?'

'Pull the other one,' Harris said. 'I'm beginning to see why twinkle-toes wanted you minded. You're a menace to society, pal.'

'Look,' Bogan rounded on the DC. 'You want to hang around like a spare prick, that's all right with me, only it's my mate up there on that bloody bridge and I'm going to get this thing sorted, got it?'

Harris spread his hands. 'Don't take it out on me, pal. I'm just here to keep you out of trouble, that's all. Besides, it's not this joker we're after, right? It's his common law we're interested in, yeah? So calm down and let's do the neighbours, see where she hangs out when she's not doing her high wire act. Fair enough?'

'I already did,' Bogan growled. 'They say she works at Nightingale's, the estate agents up town.'

'Well, why don't we get up there and talk to her mates. We can come back here later on, when we know the score. What d'you say?'

Bogan beat a fist on the door in a parting gesture. He knew Harris was right. Frustration had clouded his judgement. There was no need to dig himself in deeper just for the sake of it. The flash owner of the yellow XJS could wait.

'Yeah, you're right,' he told Harris. 'I've just got a feeling in my water about this one, that's all.'

'Comes from drinking too much coffee,' Harris laughed. 'You're too long in the tooth for that crystal ball malarky, pal.' He slapped Bogan on the shoulder in a gesture of camaraderie. 'Come on, let's see what we can find out about this bird your mate's playing footsie with. What's she called anyway?'

'Joan Jones.' Jojo answered the question, cradling Nigel in her arms. 'Silly name isn't it? Joan Elizabeth Jones, if you want the whole thing.' It sounded strange, hearing herself say her full name out loud. She'd practised it often enough, imagining herself responding to the vicar at her wedding. 'Do you, Joan Elizabeth, take this man, Michael Anthony, to your lawful wedded husband, to have and to hold . . .' Only Michael had always put it off, saying he wanted to get the business running full bore before they tied the knot. The way he had put it, it made sense. 'Trust me, Jojo,' he'd said. 'We're having fun, aren't we? Don't let's rush it. You deserve the best, princess. Only the best's good enough for my Jojo.' And like the silly cow with the silly name, she'd fallen for it because she loved him. And she'd never stopped loving him, not even when she found out he'd been shacking up with every woman who gave him the eye and squandering every penny they made on hotel suites and fancy living. Not even when Gary made his pass at her in the depth of her despair did she stop loving Michael. Her feelings ran too deep to be shut off, capped, reversed. Not even when Michael hurt her did she stop loving him. Oh, he was good at that. He would hit her where it didn't show, in the ribs, in the back, in the belly, carefully, methodically punishing her for prying into his affairs. Only Carol guessed what was happening, the days off work with a migraine or a heavy period. Carol knew the truth, but like a good friend she didn't interfere. Once in the ladies' room at the office she'd raised an eyebrow at the purple bruising which Jojo hadn't been quick enough to hide and said, 'I don't know what you and Michael are into, kiddo, and I don't want to know. If it's whips and chains turn you two on, good luck to you. Everybody to their own, I say. Take me. I mean, I wanted to race the snooker champ's motor, I'd have to dress in green baize and make him think he was potting the black. But if that bastard's getting his kicks beating you up, I'll say this once only, because it's none of my business: if he hurts you again, walk out of there, there's a couch at my place.' Jojo covered her bruises and her embarrassment, and Carol never mentioned it again.

She would look at herself in the mirror. Had she changed? Had she become the clinging shrew Michael made her out to be? Was it her fault for not giving him enough? They were questions which defied answers. More and more frequently Michael would go out drinking before he came home. She could smell the whisky on his breath, note the suffused redness of his face. One word would trigger him and he'd start in on her straight away, yelling that she was suffocating him, that he needed space to breathe. He would swing from one emotional extreme to the other, sometimes the old sparkling Michael, kind and considerate, then one slip of the tongue would spark him off, like throwing a switch on a machine. His eyes would darken and his upper lip would swell like a frog's and he would give her a beating. And through the dull spasms of pain she would wonder if he was truly mad. What was the word for a split personality—schizophrenia? She looked it up in a medical dictionary: disconnection between thoughts, feelings and action. Had she done that to him? Or had the web of deceit he had woven around them finally trapped him so that he could no longer face up to reality? More questions without answers to swirl around in her fevered mind. But through it all, not once did she ever think of leaving him. And now he was gone.

Jojo pulled herself back from her thoughts. Sitting on the girder with her legs dangling over the void, she looked down without any sensation of fear and saw her world laid out below her, the city, the river, like one of those aerial pictures on the office wall, the features which had seemed so important now tiny and insignificant. Down in the hole was how she thought of it, as she cradled the petrified kiddie-cop in her arms and said her name out loud. 'Joan Jones, I never forgave them for that silly name, my mum and dad. I hated it, even when I was a kid.' She stroked his hair, holding his face against her breasts for comfort. 'Nobody calls me that now, not for a long time. My friends all call me Jojo.'

'Jojo did what?' Carol was incredulously, crossing her legs in her tight black skirt and leaning forward to light her cigarette from the Zippo which Harris held out to her. 'You've got to be kidding.'

'No, we're pretty sure it's her,' Bogan said, sitting opposite her on the white plastic chair in the reception area of Nightingale's which was separated from the open plan office by free-standing display boards extolling the virtues of the properties currently on their books. 'That's why we're here, Mrs Cutler, to see if you can tell us why she would want to pull a crazy stunt like that.'

'Jojo?' She looked from one to the other of them. 'No, there's got to be some mistake, Jojo wouldn't say boo to a goose, you must be mixing her up with someone else.'

'We're ninety per cent positive it's her, Mrs Cutler,' Harris said. 'Otherwise we wouldn't be here bothering you.'

'You see, she's not at work here, and she's not at her flat,' Bogan said, 'so we're just making some routine inquiries. If it is your friend up there on the bridge, you'd want to help her, right?' He couldn't take his eyes off the woman's legs. She uncrossed them and then crossed them the other way, letting the skirt ride up a little.

'Let me get this straight,' Carol said. 'You're telling me Jojo climbed up on the bridge? The Arrow Bridge? Why would she want to do that?'

'That's what we thought you might be able to tell us,' Bogan said. He gave her a smile and she rewarded him, parting her lips and showing little white teeth. 'I mean, you know her, we don't. Has she been acting strangely lately?'

Carol said, 'Give me a minute, OK? You come in here and tell me Jojo's up there on the bridge. You've knocked the wind out of my sails telling me that.'

'Relax,' Bogan said. 'All we want to do is help her, so take your time. If something's happened to her—like something in the head, you know what I mean? Something tipped the balance—we just want to know, so we can work out how to deal with it.' Bogan dropped his eyes to those silky plump legs and then returned to her face. 'So you see, Carol—you don't mind if I call you Carol, do you—whatever you can tell us is going to help a lot, and I promise you anything you say will be treated in the strictest confidence.'

The tip of a pink tongue moistened her lips and then disappeared.

'For instance, what about this bloke of hers,' Harris suggested. 'This Michael Mitchell character. He's not at home either. You wouldn't happen to know where we can find him?'

Carol frowned and her eyes darkened. 'Doing his macho deep-sea diving thing, or more likely running around putting on a big show for the ladies, the creep.'

Bogan and Harris exchanged glances. 'There some problem between them?' Bogan asked.

'Look,' Carol said, taking quick nervous puffs on her cigarette, 'it's none of my business, so I didn't tell you this, right? Jojo's a nice kid, naïve and trusting—you know? I tried to tell her Michael was no good, but she wouldn't have it, she thought the sun shone out of his backside. They've been living together, what would it be, a year, year and a half, and all the time he's supposed to be going to marry her, only it never happens. Same as he's supposed to be making his first million with this diving school of his. That never happens either. You take one look at him, you can see he's all kinds of a con artist. Thinks he's God's gift, and he sure as hell pulled the wool over Jojo's eyes. For her he could do no wrong, not even when she caught him at it.'

Carol sighed. 'Yeah, well, I suppose something had to snap, the way they were going. Bastard started to knock her about. She'd come in here some days, black and blue, only even then when the writing was on the wall she wouldn't hear a word said against him. That's love and devotion for you, a whole lot of hurt.'

'You think she might have cracked up, then?' Harris said.

'I told you, I mind my own business. But I tell you something else. I wouldn't've stood for that kind of treatment, not for one minute. Go home from the office and get ten rounds in the ring for a welcome. You've got to be some kind of a masochist to put up with that. So I told her straight. I told her if she wanted my advice, she'd get out of there and forget the rat, only like I said, we just worked together, what she did in her personal life was none of my business.'

Bogan said, 'This Michael, he drive a yellow Jag, XJS convertible?'

Carol nodded. 'Flashy bastard had the works, fancy clothes, fancy car, nothing but the best. And he'd got Jojo on a piece of string.'

Bogan got up. 'Sounds like we'd better pay him a visit,' he said. 'D'you know where this diving school is?'

'Down at the marina,' Carol said, 'Dolphin Diving, that's what he calls himself. Only don't be fooled. When you meet him you wouldn't think butter'd melt in his mouth, but underneath he's got a vicious temper.' She looked up at Bogan. 'Jojo's going to be all right, isn't she?'

Bogan gave her his best smile. 'Don't worry about it, Carol, we're going to get her off there and sort out her problems. She'll be good as new.'

'One other thing . . .' Carol smoothed her skirt over her thighs.

'It's all right,' Bogan second-guessed her. 'You didn't

tell us anything, this conversation never happened. Fair enough?'

Carol half smiled. 'Actually I was going to ask you if you were interested in snooker.'

With Harris in tow, Bogan went back to the Incident Car parked on double yellows in the street outside. They got into the Montego and Bogan started the engine.

'Sounds like nothing more than a lousy domestic we've got here, boy-girl stuff,' Harris said, 'but I've got to hand it to you, pal, you've certainly got a way with the fat ladies. I could practically see the sparks. For a moment there I thought she was going to climb all over you.'

Bogan pulled out into the traffic and gunned the motor. 'It's just a gift, Dave,' he said. 'You wouldn't understand.' He glanced over at the detective lounging in the passenger's seat. 'What d'you say we go down to the waterfront and tell lover-boy his fortune. Oh and by the way, I'm not your pal.'

CHAPTER 14

'Get the Task Force out here and some traffic units to untangle that snarl-up.' Bert Royal, all business, issued his orders as he cast off the ratty Barbour and pulled on the Day-Glo jerkin with Incident Commander emblazoned on the back.

Royal was standing on the dimpled metal flooring of the command truck parked among the clutch of assorted police vehicles slewed haphazardly across the bridge approach. Slapping a fist into the palm of his hand like a prizefighter anxious for the bout to begin, Royal mentally ran down the Operations checklist for an incident on the Arrow Bridge. Task Force, Traffic Division, Communications, that would do for the first wave. Throw too much manpower at it and they'd be tripping over themselves.

'What's the Headquarters status?' he asked, rounding on Sergeant Davies who was dancing attendance.

'They've gone to passive gold, sir,' Davies informed him and Royal nodded, making another mental note. So gold control was on stand-by, but not manned up; well that suited him fine. The chain of command went bronze, silver, gold, with each step activated as the incident escalated. As on-scene commander he had assumed the silver mantle, which meant that for the time being the hierarchy was content to leave this can of worms in his hands.

Royal pulled at the lump of his nose with thumb and forefinger as he contemplated his strategy. From the moment he arrived at the bridge the crowns on his shoulders put him in charge, but he knew that he was constrained by the Ops Manual which laid down procedures for every eventuality but provided little guidance for a loony on the high steel with a kid in a policeman's uniform up there alongside her.

As if seeking some divine inspiration, Royal squinted around the bright interior of the truck which served as a mobile command post and rapped out his instructions. 'I want a sterile area. Nothing moves across the bridge either way, you got that? Seal it off.'

Davies winced. 'If they have to go around, that's a twenty-mile detour. We're already getting shunts in the tailback. Be a lot easier if we clear this lot, then start turning 'em.'

Royal chewed his lip. The Sergeant had a point, but he couldn't risk it. He shook his head. 'And we get a crunch on the span, some rubber-necker, then everything'll be fouled up. Who knows what'll touch her off.'

Davies sighed. 'Going to be a bitch, gaffer.'

'Ah, let Traffic sort it out.' Royal dismissed the problem. 'That's their headache.'

Davies put in a final plea. 'We've got an ambulance out there, medical emergency. Got a heart patient on board could snuff it any minute. They're tearing their hair.'

'OK, OK,' Royal relented. 'Give 'em an escort and let 'em across, but no sirens, understood?'

Davies looked uneasy. 'There's worse. Chris Carpenter's out there, our favourite MP. Throwing his weight around, screaming he's got an urgent appointment. Says he'll have my stripes if I don't get him across that bridge pronto.'

Royal smiled. 'Well, you be sure to give Mr Loudmouth Carpenter my respects, then kick his arse out of it like the rest.' Tightening his jaw, he said, 'And if he gives you any more flak, Davies, you can tell him we've got an officer from Complaints and Discipline right here if he wants to make something of it.' He inclined his head towards Vicky Rivers over at the radio console.

Davies blanched. 'Er, I think you ought to know, sir, last time I saw him, a minute ago, he was calling the chief on his car phone and looked like he was going to burst a blood vessel.'

'I don't care if he's on the phone to the freaking Pope,' Royal snapped. 'He can walk on water for all I care, but he's not crossing that bridge, and that's final. What else?'

Davies shrugged. 'Just a mess of crunched bumpers, bust headlights and short tempers.'

'All right.' Royal was anxious to move on. 'Get on to Alpha Victor—' he used the radio code for Headquarters —'tell 'em to put out an all-media appeal to stay away from the bridge.'

'Bay Metro'll be climbing the wall, traffic's on a knife edge as it is, something like this and everything's going to grind to a standstill.'

'Well, the town hall's just going to have to lump it,' Royal said. He glanced at Vicky and lowered his voice. 'Where's Bogan?'

'He skipped out while I had my hands full.' Davies looked peeved. 'Chasing up a line on the lady.'

'Get him on the bat phone,' Royal instructed. 'I want him back here, right away, and that's an order.'

Although it was the size of a pantechnicon, racks of emergency equipment gave the interior of the windowless command truck a cramped, utilitarian feel, rather like the bowels of a wartime submarine, Royal thought as he threaded his way through the gaggle of specialists in lurid jackets similar to his own who were busy setting up the COMCON computer link, the hele-tele and the multi-track recorders. At a pull-down workstation Vicky Rivers was checking the radio console as a comms operator threw the switches, searching the bands for the UHF portable Nigel Wilcox had taken aloft.

As Royal came up behind her, she turned and eyed him resentfully, still smarting from the episode at the Trade Winds. In the company of the truck's technical crew Royal would do her the courtesy of observing the formalities befitting her rank, and ignoring her petulant look he told her briskly, 'As it stands we're holding on silver, but gold's up and raring to go the minute we fumble the ball, so let's see if we can't show Headquarters a clean pair of heels on this one, Inspector. You think you're up to it?'

Vicky winced at a sudden blast of static as the scanner hopped channels. 'Well, at least the PC's got a portable, so we should be able to keep it in the family. Soon as we're locked on, I'll give him the wake-up call.'

'Go easy on him, Vicky,' Royal said. 'He's a good lad, but he's still wet behind the ears.'

'I got his profile off Sergeant Davies,' Vicky said. 'When I sweet talk him, he'll think I'm his mother. How're we doing on his lady-friend?'

'Working on it,' Royal said. 'Should have her ID'd any minute now.'

'Sooner the better.' Vicky frowned. 'The way these things go, the first few minutes are the worst. Once we've got a dialogue going we can settle down into the routine.'

'Oh, you've done this before?'

'Only in the training school,' Vicky admitted, a defensive smile twitching her lips. 'So you see, I'm as green as young Nigel up there, only I don't aim to let it show.'

Royal patted her shoulder. It was a clumsy gesture, but he wanted to boost her confidence, let her know with a touch and a glance that she didn't have to prove anything as far as he was concerned. 'Just take it nice and easy,' he murmured gruffly, 'nobody's expecting miracles.'

As he spoke a draught caught his neck and he turned to witness the scene as the rear door was flung back and a uniform appeared in the opening making a grandstand entrance, the face split in a cocky grin.

'Her name's Joan Jones,' Bogan announced as he bounded up the metal steps and burst into the command truck, 'only everybody calls her Jojo.' He ignored Davies who was trying to head him off and confronted Bert Royal.

'Got a fancy pad over in Bosun's Reach where she lives with her boyfriend, character by the name of Michael Mitchell, runs his own diving school down at the marina. We looked all over for him, only he's nowhere to be found. Could be he's taken a powder.'

Royal felt his chest tighten. Standing between Bogan and Vicky, he felt as though he was on the high wire himself as the two came face to face for the first time.

'Could be a domestic, gaffer,' the unwitting subject of the rubber heel's ire continued his report. 'According to the neighbours and her friends at work they hadn't been hitting it off too well of late.'

Royal cleared his throat as he stepped to one side and made the introductions. 'This is Inspector Rivers, giving us a hand from Headquarters, she's the negotiator.' He saw the surprise in Bogan's expression as he heard himself explain to Vicky, 'PC Bogan here is Wilcox's crewmate.' And then back to Bogan, grinding it out: 'We want to know what this is all about from square one and we don't have any time to waste, so you'd better brief us on the details right now.' His tone grew bleak, and although he addressed himself to Bogan his words were intended for both of them. 'There's no room here for prima donnas, we're just going to buckle down and get the job done, understood?'

Their eyes met and there was an instant spark of animosity. Vicky recognized the sly look on Bogan's face as he continued the story in a matter-of-fact tone. His slippery gaze travelled from head to toe and she felt him mentally undressing her, the usual macho response she had experienced so many times before in her male-dominated world that she had become inured to the blatant sexual challenge. But Bogan's eyes disturbed her. There was something else there, behind the lechery: that shut-down, closed-off arrogance of the old-time street cop. The hair at the nape of her neck tingled. It was her father's look.

Bogan appraised the lady from up-town without bothering to hide his disdain. Skirts in the job were just a political gesture, an irrelevance. Usually they turned out to be dogs, dykes or hard-faced bitches trying to muscle in on man's work. This one intrigued him, though. Pretty little thing with a nice firm body, and if she'd made inspector she must've been putting it out to one of the gaffers on the top corridor. All the same, there was something about her which struck a chord in his memory, reminded him of someone. Give it time and it'd come back to him.

High on the Arrow Bridge Nigel knew he was hallucinating. The red iron latticework came alive, buckled and undulated before his eyes, girders swayed, bolt heads bulged, as if the whole malevolent structure seemed determined to shrug him off his precarious perch. The river crooned up to him, low and soothing, encouraging him to end his ordeal with the long swallow dive. A plastic parrot on his shoulder began to squawk.

'OK, Nigel, time we had a talk.' The parrot mimicked a woman's voice which spoke softly to him. 'Take it easy now, nice and easy, nothing to get excited about. My name's Vicky and I'm your friend, Nigel, I'm going to take care of you and the little lady up there. Only you're going to have to help me, OK? I just want you to press the button and let me know you're both OK. Can you do that for me, Nigel?'

Nigel's head reeled as he clung desperately to the woman. The talking parrot had flown up to torment him and he could feel its talons digging into his shoulder. He cringed away from it, and Jojo stroked his hair. 'There, there,' she murmured, 'it's going to be all right. It's just your friends down there getting restless.'

'Don't let it—' Nigel gasped, burrowing his face into the fabric, listening to her heartbeat—'don't let it get me!'

'Hey, come on,' Jojo said, smoothing his hair, 'I'm here. It's going to be all right, nothing's going to get you.'

Nigel gagged, pawed at his shoulder. She didn't understand.

Jojo cradled his head. 'Come on, sweetie, take a look. There's no parrot. It's that radio thing on your shoulder-strap. They want to talk to you down there, that's all it is. It's nothing.'

But Nigel was too far gone. 'Please . . . please, Jojo,' he pleaded, 'don't let the parrot get me!'

In the command truck Vicky pressed the mute and turned to Royal. 'I can't get any sense out of him.' She lifted the headset, tossed her hair and frowned. 'I could be wrong, but I reckon our Nigel's bitten off more than he can chew. He show any stress symptoms?'

At Royal's elbow Bogan said, 'No way, Nigel's all right. Let me talk to him, I'll soon straighten him out.'

He moved forward but Royal stopped him. 'I don't get it,' Vicky said. 'One minute he's rational, then he's talking gibberish.' She gave her head another puzzled shake. 'I can't get through to him. If he doesn't snap out of it in a minute, we're going to have a problem.'

Bogan grew agitated. 'Let me talk to him, gaffer, I'll soon kick him into gear.'

'You stay out of it, Bogan,' Royal snapped, weighing up the situation. 'If he hears you yelling in his ear he's going to flip completely. You want to do something useful, take the binos and go outside and have a squint. See if you can see what he's up to.' He turned to Vicky. 'Try the woman,' he said, 'give her some girl-talk.'

With the powerful binoculars in his hand, Bogan turned to leave the truck. He squeezed past a huddle over a drop-down table strewn with blueprints of the bridge. The hulking maintenance foreman was at the centre of the group tracing a stubby finger over the architect's drawing as though he was casting the runes, a deep frown creasing his forehead. 'Then of course we could try C gantry which goes from here and cuts across the structure, only it's just as bad as the other way. She's going to see us coming a mile off.'

A Task Force inspector pushed a cowlick of hair from his eyes. 'What if we play for time, wait until it gets dark and then sneak up on her?'

The burly foreman gave him a scornful look. 'You'd have to be out of your mind to go up there in the dark. I've been a steeplejack all my life, and I tell you I've got a healthy respect for that old bridge. Nothing, and I mean nothing, would get me up there in the dark, it'd be plain suicide.' He folded his arms across his barrel chest and left the word hanging ominously in the air.

Consumed with frustration, Bogan jumped out of the truck, went over to the rail and raised the binoculars. The structure leaped into close-up as he focused the glasses and began to traverse the ironwork. Higher he went until he could pick them out, two figures huddled together on a fork below the cable. But from this perspective the cross-member obscured them from view and all he could make out were their legs dangling in space. Even with his feet planted firmly on the bridge the disembodied sensation of peering through the powerful lenses made Bogan dizzy and he lowered the binoculars and held on to the rail to steady himself. Come on, Nige! He almost shouted out loud as helplessness gnawed at him. Get on with it! He tried to rationalize it. That silly bitch must've gone soft in the head, telling him Nigel had frozen up there. No, no way could he accept that. No partner of Ted Bogan's ever cracked up, not even the carrot-top. It just wasn't possible.

Bogan raised the binoculars again and trained them on the spot, willing Nigel to screw his courage to the sticking-point and start leading the crazy cow down so that they could wrap this thing up. The kid was probably just spinning it out while she told him her life-story. Bending her ear with all that sociology crap they filled their heads with these days. 'Come on, Nige!' Bogan muttered under his breath, 'stop mucking about . . . you're making me look a right prat down here.' But despite his desperate attempt at extra-sensory communication, in the bright ring of the binoculars the legs hung motionless.

At the sound of angry voices Bogan spun around to see what was going on behind him. There was some sort of commotion at the barricade which had been hastily thrown across the bridge approach to keep the gawpers at bay. Behind the interlocking metal gates a crowd had gathered and an ice-cream van was plying a healthy trade. The disturbance had been caused by the growing press corps which had slipped the leash and burst through the barricades pursued by a couple of flustered minders.

A TV reporter with a familiar pepper-and-salt mane towing a tracksuited cameraman with a Betacam bouncing on his shoulder stepped out of the stampede and began to talk into a cellphone. 'Yeah, Andy . . . yeah, yeah, that's what they're saying, some rookie disobeyed orders, went up alone and now he's lost his bottle. You got that chopper up yet?'

Unable to contain himself, Bogan grabbed the man's arm as he dashed past and swung him around, pushing his face into his. 'Where'd you hear that?'

The TV reporter tossed his perm. 'Couple of your guys back there were talking about it.' He gestured towards the barricade.

'Well, they're just shooting their stupid mouths off,' Bogan snarled, outrage welling up inside him. 'That kid up there's a hero.'

'Oh yeah?' The reporter didn't look convinced.

'You can take it from me,' Bogan said, recalling the name from the TV screen. He could picture him saying, This is Bob Costello, *Eyewitness News*. 'I ought to know, I'm his partner.'

Perking up, Costello retrieved his arm. 'You don't say? Hey, can we get this on camera?'

Bogan looked at the cameraman who was already focusing his electronic proboscis as Costello manœuvred himself so that the shot took in the superstructure of the bridge. 'Your lot are just giving us the runaround,' he protested. 'Wouldn't even give us a pool.' He glanced quickly across at the rampaging horde which was now being unceremoniously rounded up. 'I mean, we're just doing our job, so how're we supposed to get it right if nobody'll talk to us?' A hooded mike appeared in his hand and he nodded to the cameraman. 'Ready, John, turn over and let's make it a quickie.' The tracksuit crouched slightly and thrust the black eye of the lens towards Bogan's face. 'Running,' he muttered, 'speed.'

Costello turned to Bogan. 'Give me a sound level. Tell me your name.'

'Bogan,' Bogan said, 'PC Ted Bogan.'

'Just look at me,' Costello instructed, 'forget the camera, Ted. Just for the record, what's your partner's name?'

'PC Wilcox,' Bogan said. 'Nigel Wilcox.'

'And he's up there on the bridge?'

Bogan nodded, the fat sheath of the mike under his nose.

'OK, Ted, we're running,' Costello said. 'Tell me what happened here in your own words.'

Bogan glanced at the camera. It had a sticker on the side, a big blue eye with the words *Eyewitness News*. He looked back at Costello who was nodding and smiling encouragingly.

'Well, Bob,' Bogan said, 'we're the Incident Car crew, me and Nigel—PC Wilcox. We were on patrol when a guy came running up the street and flagged us down, turned out to be one of the guys off the tolls. He told us there was a woman climbing up the bridge there. We shot over and we could see her going up the tower, and Nigel—PC Wilcox—went up after her. That was it, we could see she was in trouble, so he went up after her.'

'A pretty brave thing to do,' Costello said.

Bogan said, 'Well, that was Nigel all over. I said I'd go

up as I was the senior man, but he wouldn't hear of it, said he was younger and fitter than me, and he could climb quicker. He didn't hesitate, he just went up there.'

'He was taking a risk, wasn't he?' Costello injected a little breathlessness into the question for dramatic effect.

'Look, Bob,' Bogan said, 'we're police officers, what you'd call taking risks is all part of the job for us. Mostly you don't have time to worry about it, it's like a reflex, you just do it. Nigel—er PC Wilcox—saw a damsel in distress and just naturally did what he had to do even if it meant risking his own life, but that's what it's all about Bob, that's what we get paid to do.'

He glanced at the camera, then back to Costello, and dropped his voice to a confidential tone. 'Nigel wouldn't thank me for saying this, he's too modest, but as far as I'm concerned, that kid up there's all kinds of a hero. The people of this city ought to be proud they've got fine young officers like Nigel Wilcox willing to risk their hide to protect them. If you ask me, he deserves a medal.'

Costello smiled. This was good gritty stuff. 'Do you know who the woman is?'

Bogan sidestepped the question. 'I'm just a PC, Bob, I don't have the authority to release that kind of information. You'll have to call the press office.'

'Well, what d'you think made her do it?'

Bogan shrugged eloquently. 'Why do normal people do crazy things? Who knows what goes through their minds?'

Costello shot a glance to where the rest of the media had been corralled on the far side of the bridge and were being herded back to the barricade. One of the minders was bearing down on them.

'Wrap it, John,' he told the cameraman, 'no time for cutaways, the stormtrooper's coming.' To Bogan he said, 'That was just great, Ted, great story. We're going to get Nigel that medal.' He slipped a card into Bogan's hand.

'The mobile number's on there, give me a ring, OK? We'd better run if we're going to make the bulletin.' He patted Bogan's shoulder, 'Keep in touch, OK?'

Bogan slipped the card into his pocket and watched as the star of *Eyewitness News* was hustled back behind the barricade. The minder, a chief inspector from Headquarters, came across, looking flustered. 'Bloody vultures,' he protested. 'They've been told not to talk to individual officers. What'd he want?'

Still smarting from the injustice of reflected criticism, Bogan looked the minder in the eye and replied, 'Said he's doing the Food Show, sir, so I gave him my grannie's recipe for stuffed pork.'

Just at that moment Sergeant Davies came out of the command truck, his face grey. He leaned on the rail and took in gulps of air, breathing deeply. 'I had to get out of that madhouse,' he confided in Bogan, 'get a breath of fresh air.' His head sagged miserably. 'The way the heavy mob's carrying on in there, you'd think they were going up the north face of the bloody Eiger.' He sucked in more deep breaths, then shaded his eyes with a hand and stared up at the bridge. 'You see anything?'

Bogan said, 'Not with all that junk in the way.'

'Well,' Davies sighed, 'I hate to say this, Bogan, but your mate's really messed up. You want to hear my private nightmare? We've got a loony up there all right, only it's the other way around.' His moustache quivered as he abandoned the party line and tried to placate the old-timer by falling back on the canteen doctrine. 'We both know why? No policemanship any more. Ninety per cent of our strength on the streets these days are kids who don't have the sense to get in out of the rain. Toytown cops. Oh, the lady'll steal the show, but your mate's the real victim.'

Enraged, Bogan grabbed the dapper sergeant by the lapels. 'Don't give me that bullshit.' He lifted Davies off his feet. 'Maybe that was a green kid you foisted on me this morning, but now he's my crewmate. Any more snide cracks and so help me, I'll chuck you over.' He nodded towards the rail.

CHAPTER 15

The third deck of the Wharf Street multi-storey car park was in semi-darkness. The strip lighting had long since been ripped from the low ceiling and the walls, already blackened with grime, were daubed with morbid graffiti which drew heavily on bodily functions.

The place resembled a dismal concrete cave in which dwelt the rusting hulks of old bangers, scorned even by the vandals. Like a colt entering the knacker's yard, the yellow XJS came up the ramp with a squeal of tyres, shied at the tight curve and had to be spurred into the deep shadow between the pillars.

Flopped in the passenger's seat, Woody told Phil to cut the engine. Into the silence he said, 'Nice wheels, maybe I'll drop a line to *What Car*, give 'em my vote on getaway car of the year.'

Phil looked around. 'Seems a pity to ditch it in this pisshole.'

Woody said, 'What've you got in mind, genius?'

'I dunno why we don't take it down to Eddie's yard, get him to strip it and make a few quid.'

'Because it's hot, dummy,' Woody said. 'Any other brilliant suggestions?'

Phil shot a glance at the girl in the back. She gave him a pouty smile and he felt elated, coming back on to a high now that the danger was over.

'We could always pull another job,' he suggested, feeling cocky. 'Give me a go with the shooter. You can drive.'

Woody put his head back on the rest and laughed. His adam's apple bobbed. 'Listen to the bad bandit. You practically filled your pants back there.'

But Phil was staring at the girl giving him the come-on

from the back seat. Suddenly he became consumed with the notion of consummating the robbery by ravaging her right there on the Jag's cream hide upholstery. After all, she'd promised him a treat.

Catching the signs, Woody said over his shoulder, 'I think hot rod fancies you, Sonia. Show him your tits.'

The girl pulled up her T-shirt and Phil took a look at her breasts. He was instantly aroused. 'You going to be a mate, Woody—' excitement cracked his voice— 'take a walk or something while me and Sonia christen this motor.'

'Hear that?' Woody chuckled. 'Oh, our Phil's got a hard-on for you all right, Sonia. What d'you say, do you want to let him have it?'

'Oh yeah.' The girl breathed the words. 'Oh, I really do.' She leaned forward and rubbed a nipple against the seat back.

Phil's eyes bulged, he couldn't believe his luck. He became so preoccupied with his fantasy that he was caught off guard by the sinewy arm which pinned him to the seat as Woody lunged across the car, his face twisted into a leer. He jerked open Phil's jeans, thrust his hand inside, grabbed his erection and jerked him off. Phil was aware of his own warm juice trickling down his leg as he tried to wriggle free, but Woody pushed him back.

'Feeling better, hard man?'

'You bastard!' Phil cried out, tears of humiliation welling in his eyes. 'You bastard!'

'A wank's all he's worth,' the girl sneered in her baby doll voice. Woody shot her a warning glance. 'Put 'em away, Sonia,' he told her coldly and she pulled down the T-shirt in a huff and sank back into the seat.

'Here's your wages.' Woody tossed a fistful of notes into Phil's sticky lap and picked up the shotgun. He held the stubby barrels against the driver's head. 'Now get lost if you don't want to chase your brains around the roof.'

Phil reached down between his legs and his hand closed

around the handle of the knife under the seat. For a second, rage emboldened him, but the merciless challenge in the other man's eyes broke his nerve. He got out of the car, stuffing the money into his pockets. The girl was watching him, a feral gleam in her eye. 'Bye-bye, Phil,' she called out.

Laughter echoed after him as Phil clattered down the stairwell and into the street. Inflamed with impotent rage, he wished he'd had the guts to stick Woody with the knife, then turn the blade on the little teaser and rip her open. He could see himself doing it, blood spattering Woody's stupid bandanna, the girl squealing as the knife went into her soft belly. Gorged on blood lust, he didn't stop to wonder how that knife had simply materialized in his hand, but yearned only to use it. Walking to the street corner, heading back to where his Cortina was parked nearby, Phil vented his frustration by kicking a telephone kiosk which had already been vandalized. From one of the intact glass panels, a sticker which had survived the wreckers caught his eye. A ruddy-faced British bulldog in a Union Jack waistcoat was pointing a finger at him, mouthing a slogan. Phil read the phone number underneath the caricature and his lip curled. He pulled open the door of the kiosk and went inside. The fittings had been torn out, but miraculously the armour-plated telephone was still intact. Without pausing to contemplate the consequences, he picked up the phone and dialled the number, soaring on a heady thermal of revenge.

Jojo was growing tired, her concentration slipping. She had watched the sun traverse the expanse of sky until now in the late afternoon its warmth diminished and the chill of approaching dusk weakened her resolve. She looked down and saw the bridge choked with miniature vehicles with black numerals on their white roofs, the scene resembling some board game she could reach out and play from her perch high on the superstructure. Wisps of mist were drifting up from the river in weird shapes and the parrot lying in her lap crooned softly, adding a sound track to the surreal movie playing before her eyes. Ever since Nigel's terrified outburst she had thought of it as the parrot, the radio microphone she had unclipped from his epaulette and concealed within the folds of her own clothing to pacify him. He still clung to her, his head against her shoulder, but his eyes were closed and his voice which muttered disjointed phrases had grown listless and she had the feeling that he was withdrawing into himself little by little. At some time, when she judged it was right, she had decided that she would remove his belt and handcuffs and use them to lash him to the girder so that he would be safe. In the meantime the parrot kept talking to her.

'Joan? Come on, Joan.' Insistent, never letting up. 'I know you can hear me, so why don't you talk to me, eh? It's easy, jut press the button on the side of the microphone there and talk to me. How about it, Joan?' The woman's voice was calm, reasonable, soothing. Sounded like her mom, she thought, full of worldly wisdom she didn't want to hear.

'Joan, you be in by midnight, you hear, you know what your father's like if you're out till all hours.'

'But, Mom, the party doesn't start till nine . . .'

'What kind of a party's that? We didn't bring you up to go to parties half the night. Your father . . . you know . . . every time you're out late he's thinking some boy's pawing you, getting you into trouble. Nice girls don't go to parties like that, Joan.'

'We're just going to play some music, Mom, that's all. It's not an orgy or anything and besides I'm old enough to look after myself. What's the matter, don't you trust me?'

'You know your father . . . he's worried about you, that's all. Just promise me you'll be home by midnight.'

'Dad, Dad, Dad this, Dad that. I'm sick of what Dad

wants. Anybody'd think I'll turn into a pumpkin. I don't know why you married him.'

'Don't you give me any lip, my girl. Midnight, not a minute later.'

The parrot butted in. 'How about it, Joan? Talk to me. I only want to help you, that's a promise. You don't have to do anything, just talk. Tell me what this is all about, Joan, and I can help you. Nothing's black as it looks, you know that, don't you. Look, whatever it is, we can work something out, but I can't help unless you tell me about it. I'm your friend, Joan, you've got to believe that. So how about it, eh? Just press the button and say something . . . please, Joan.'

The motherly voice, so soothing, so wise. Joan held the parrot in her hand and stared at its black plastic plumage. So sweet and considerate, what did she know? How could a parrot help her now? Sprout wings and they could fly away together? She looked at Nigel's face. It was in repose, the lips moving soundlessly as he journeyed into some private world, blanched white like her mother's face as she sat helplessly beside her bed in the hospice and watched the life drain out of her until she was gone to join her father in the graveyard. Then she was alone.

Irrational fury exploded the dreamlike sequence and Jojo pressed the button on the side of the mike and cut the sweet voice off. 'Don't call me Joan!' she shouted down her tormentor. 'Don't you ever call me that. My name's Jojo.'

'Holy shit!' Bogan yelled releasing the sergeant and craning into the sky. 'Where the hell did that come from?'

Davies danced clear of Bogan's clutches and followed the PC's gaze. 'Jesus,' he yelped, 'what's that maniac think he's doing?' The sudden roar overhead grew to a thunder. 'Look out! He's going to hit the bloody bridge!'

The red and white helicopter which appeared out of nowhere to make a barnstorming run down the river flashed over the Arrow Bridge with a deafening clatter of rotors, heeled into a stuttering turn and swung back for another pass. The side of the Jetranger was open and a cameraman was hanging out on a despatcher's harness. The machine shuddered into a hover and began to claw its way along the superstructure of the bridge.

Bert Royal appeared in the doorway of the command truck, his face frantic. 'Get that chopper out of here!' he shouted at Davies. 'I thought we'd got air exclusion on this!' He stabbed a finger at the helicopter which was hanging over the bridge like an inquisitive dragonfly. 'I'll have that lunatic's licence. Get him out of here!'

Hopping from foot to foot, the luckless sergeant spoke urgently into his portable. 'What d'you expect me to bloody well do?' he vented his frustration, his reverence for rank temporarily suspended. 'Shoot the fucker down?'

From the doorway of the truck Royal gave him a flinty stare. 'Get ours up there and chase him off, Sergeant, before I get really annoyed. Tell 'em to throw the book at him.'

Davies, his face sweaty, spoke rapidly into the radio while Bogan watched the Jetranger perform its intricate ballet around the ironwork of the bridge. For a moment the rotor scythed dangerously near the superstructure and it looked as if the cameraman hanging from the open door would somehow scoop the two figures from their perch. Bogan held his breath.

The minder came running up with Bob Costello in tow. The TV reporter confronted Bert Royal, transfixed in the doorway, and fluffed his perm self-importantly.

'I already told him he's buggering a police operation, sir,' the minder started to explain, but Costello cut him short, puffing out his chest. 'Superintendent,' he addressed Royal with a grandoise sweep of his arm, 'I have the authority of *Eyewitness News* to place our helicopter at your disposal.'

From the top step of the truck Royal looked down on the

famous face and felt a volcano inside him about to erupt. 'Get him out of my sight,' he told the Inspector in a strangled rasp. 'Lock him up for obstruction.'

A collective gasp went up from the crowd like a sigh of breeze and Bogan swept the binoculars up and spotted the object of their excitement. 'Here come the flying leathernecks,' some wag sang out as the police helicopter skimmed down the river and promptly engaged the other machine in a dogfight with both pilots testing each other's skills. They spiralled away from the bridge, gaining height, the cameraman still filming, and then the Jetranger broke away from the aerial game of tag and headed back over the city.

His face a grim mask, Royal called them together in the command truck. 'We're losing the initiative—' his words were a flat monotone— 'I just had gold on the horn wanting to know what the hell we're playing at.' He looked around the group. 'He told me in no uncertain terms to end this pantomime before we become a laughing-stock.' He ran a hand over his pate. 'And just for good measure, the weather's closing in, mist coming off the river. If we leave it much longer we won't be able to see a hand in front of our face, so like it or not, this is crunch time. I'm putting men on the towers, three on each. Just as it gets dusk, Inspector Rivers will distract the woman and we'll jump her.' He looked around the gathered ranks defiantly, feeling the lone decision of command weigh heavily on his shoulders, then continued gruffly, 'Oh, and I've requested an MDP launch to sit under the bridge in case we have to fish anyone out.' His gaze met their eyes, warning off any dissent. 'OK, let's get going.'

In the crush a Task Force man squeezed in beside Bogan and muttered *sotto voce*, 'I bet he drinks Carling Black label.'

Royal came over, looking pained. 'You'd better track down the boyfriend fast, Bogan, he's the only ace left in the pack.'

From across the crowded truck a comms operator called out, waving a phone and Bogan went over. 'DC Harris wants you,' he said.

Bogan took the handset with a raise of the eyebrow. 'You ready for this, pal?' The detective sounded chirpy. 'You know that Jag you circulated? Yellow soft-top. It's popped up again.'

Bogan said, 'Where?'

'Multi-storey down in the rats' nest. Some toe-rag called *Crimestoppers* and told us where we could find it, gave your name.'

'My name?'

Harris chuckled. 'And that's not the best bit, pal. It's the same motor clocked on the Luxton blagging. Looks like our friend's putting it about a bit.'

'What's the score now?' Bogan asked.

'The lads are sitting on it,' Harris said, 'in case he comes back for more fun and games. You want to go down?'

Bogan thought about it. Then he said, 'Yeah, why not . . . No, wait a minute—' Another idea had come to him. 'Suspicion of armed robbery, that's good grounds for a warrant, isn't it?'

'Hundred per cent,' Harris agreed.

'Get one then, seeing as you're such a stickler for detail, and we'll give his drum a spin first. The Jag'll keep. I'll see you there.' Bogan hung up the phone.

Paul hung up the phone. He came out of the booth in the foyer of the office block where they'd been filling in time doing credit checks and told Russ: 'Ron just had a call from a mate of his in the force, the one he keeps sweet, told him they've traced the banana split.'

'Where?' Russ asked, his eyes widening.

Paul fiddled with the pager which had bleeped him to call the office. 'Wharf Street multi-storey, sitting there large as life.' He jabbed Russ in the chest. 'So you get a chance to atone for your sins. Come on, let's get weaving before it does the vanishing act again. You got the spare set of keys?'

'In my pocket,' Russ said, checking to be sure.

'Good, because if we snatch it back this time, we make sure it stays snatched, got it? I won't tell you what Ron said he'll do to you if you balls it up again, it might put you off your stroke.'

As they drove across town Paul turned on the radio and caught the end of a newsflash on Metro Sound. A breathless girl reporter was saying: 'Emergency services still seem powerless to intervene in the drama which has gripped the city all day. Tension mounted a moment ago when two helicopters circled the bridge, fuelling speculation that a rescue bid was being mounted. But no attempt seems to have been made to reach the mystery woman perched high on the girder, although I understand a negotiator has tried to talk her down as yet without success. As for the police officer up there with her, we know only that he risked his own life to reach her side in the opening moments of this unfolding drama, now watched by a huge crowd gathered at the bridge. But we're right here at the scene, and we'll bring you updates as they happen. This is Debbie Dee at the Arrow Bridge for Metro news.'

Paul said, 'Beats me where they get 'em from, sounds like she's practically having an orgasm.'

'Probably thinks she's Kate Adie, wetting her knickers on the big one,' Russ said.

'Got to be some crackpot stunt,' Paul said. 'Greenpeace or something, climb a bridge and save a whale. I dunno why they give those freaks free publicity. We want that kind of air time, we've got to pay for it through the nose.'

Russ looked at him. 'You want to climb the bridge?'

'Shit, no,' Paul said. 'That kind of crazy stunt can be a serious risk to your health.'

They threaded down into the docks, passed through a wasteland of railway sidings and turned into Wharf Road.

Paul parked opposite the multi-storey. Looking through the windscreen, he could see a bunch of kids kicking a beer can up the street. From the doorway of a derelict shop boarded up with corrugated iron another group watched dull-eyed.

Russ sensed the electric tingle of suppressed violence in the rundown district. He swallowed hard. 'Why don't we drive up?' he suggested nervously.

'Nah, better I stay here and watch points,' Paul said. He looked at Russ. 'Don't tell me you've got the wind up again.'

Russ stared into the gloom of the car park. 'I just thought it'd be quicker, that's all.'

'And what if these little tearaways block off the exit just for a bit of sport? We'd be up the creek. I'll stay here and make sure you've got a clear run.'

'Bloody snatchbacks,' Russ muttered. 'I hate doing this.'

'It'll only take a tick,' Paul said. 'All you've got to do is get in there, go up to the third level, make sure the coast's clear and drive it out. Jesus Christ, Russ, do I have to hold your hand all the time?'

Stung into action by the rebuke, Russ got out of the Orion and crossed the road to the car park. At the dingy cavern of the entrance he glanced back once. The ginger Garfield was grinning at him from the rear window of the car.

The stairwell stank of urine and Russ wrinkled his nose and took the stairs two at a time. When he reached the third deck he was out of breath, but the place felt so creepy that he didn't pause, just walked rapidly down the aisle between the pillars, averting his eyes from the deep pools of shadow and was mightily relieved to see the banana split up ahead. With the keys in his hand he trotted the last few yards, his heart pounding vigorously, took a quick glance inside the Jag to make sure it was empty, opened the door and jumped inside. He was leaning forward fumbling with the key in the ignition when dark shapes suddenly materialized from the gloom. As he looked up, his eyes bulged in panic. The men who appeared from nowhere wore flak jackets and ski caps and thrust Heckler and Koch carbines towards the Jaguar. 'Freeze, armed police!' one of them yelled. 'Don't even think about it.' Hands yanked him out and pinned him to the car. 'Hey, what is this?' Russ yelped. They mobbed him, pulled his arms back and he heard the rasp of the ratchets as the handcuffs went on. In his ear a voice said, 'Are you kidding, shitbrain? You're under arrest for armed robbery!'

Russ was too stunned to protest. His chest felt tight and his mouth flapped soundlessly. As they frogmarched him to their van he heard one of them say, 'What about the motor, Sarge?'

'Leave it,' came the reply, 'SOCO's coming out to pick it up.'

CHAPTER 16

The light was fading into murky dusk when the six Task Force volunteers blacked up and began to scale the towers. In the command truck Vicky Rivers had almost exhausted her repertoire. Under the harsh lights her face looked gaunt and haggard, but those Jack Rivers eyes still smouldered with dogged determination. She had talked herself out fearing that the batteries in the police issue Motorola must be fading by now. The woman hadn't responded to her entreaties for a while and she was no longer sure that she could even hear her, yet still she persevered, adjusting the stalk mike for the last throw, perversely hoping that Bogan would turn up the elusive Michael Mitchell.

'Jojo? How're you doing, Jojo? . . . Look, it's going to get dark and cold in a minute and that's going to make it hard for me to help you. I know I keep saying this, but it's the truth, you need a friend right now, and I'm going to be here for you, Jojo, whatever it takes. It can't be so bad we can't work it out, you and me. I'm your friend, Jojo.' Static hissed into the silence. 'Look, I tell you what I'll do—' Vicky offered up a silent prayer. 'To prove to you I'm your friend, I'll get Michael to talk to you.'

'Michael?' The name bounced back from the hiss. Reception was weak and Vicky reached out to fine-tune the set, her spirits rising.

'Yeah, Michael,' she said. 'Michael's worried about you, Jojo, all your friends are, but particularly Michael.'

'Michael's there? My Michael?'

'He's coming right now, Jojo, he's on the way.' Vicky grabbed at the straw. 'He's worried sick, he just wants you down here, safe and sound. He'll be here any minute, so why don't you come down and see for yourself. Just say the word.'

Silence.

'Come on, Jojo,' Vicky pleaded. 'Do it for Michael, what d'you say?'

Michael? The parrot said Michael. Jojo stared at the microphone in her hand. She wanted to believe the voice, but she couldn't bring herself to give in. It was ironic, all this time she'd ached to follow him, catch him up, tell him that she loved him and they could start again, and now he was going to turn up out of nowhere. That was typical of Michael.

Jojo looked down. A purple haze was gathering, drawing a diaphanous veil over the Lilliput city stretched out at her feet. The mist rose in layers, tendrils reaching up like grasping hands. Lights were coming on, blurred in the thickening soup, extinguished one by one, like the flicker of fallen stars. She turned her eyes upwards and stared into the sky. It was lighter up there, but the horizon had disappeared into the murk. Like looking up a shaft, right above her she saw contrails cut a pink-tinged swathe across the heavens, the tiny arrowhead of the westbound jet just visible. The first clammy finger caressed her face like the kiss of death.

Jojo got down into herself, worked at it. All she wanted was to get below the thing that troubled her, but it always came back, fluttering in her face like raven's wings, following her down, frightening her. Cramps twitched low in her stomach as she twisted and turned, trying to outrun the demon of her nightmare.

Michael! Hearing the parrot squawk his name had thrown her out of kilter. Deep down the tunnel of her subconscious a door she had been holding shut suddenly bucked against her hands. Michael was coming . . . coming to talk to her . . . talk her down off the bridge. She shook her head . . . no, please, no . . . pushed against the door with all her might, but the force on the other side was too strong for her. The door flew open . . .

Michael, casual in a mustard-coloured polo shirt and charcoal moleskin slacks walked into the living-room, dumped his wetsuit across an easy chair and went for the whisky bottle on the sideboard in the dining alcove. He was already nasty drunk, his face puffed and blotched, his eyes small and mean. Jojo read the signs from the kitchen doorway as she turned from the hob where she was putting the final touches to their supper, *spaghetti con melanzane*, covering the eggplant with tomato sauce. She knew better than to tangle with him in this ugly mood, but as he stumbled against the oval gateleg knocking the wine she had already poured over the linen tablecloth, the sight of him just snapped her self-control.

She came out of the kitchen, a cloth balled in her fist, hot tears starting in her eyes. 'Look what you've done, you stupid shit.'

Michael picked up the Bell's and took a long swig from the bottle. His eyes were bloodshot and he turned with a look of surprise on his face as though seeing her for the first time.

Jojo began dabbing at the spilled wine with the cloth. 'Look what you've done you clumsy shit, you've ruined it, I'll never get this out.'

Michael didn't say anything. He put the bottle down, stepped over and hit her in the face with the back of his hand. Jojo felt her teeth rattle as the slap threw her against the wall. Michael was after her, grabbed her blouse and tore it off, hitting her another open-handed blow which knocked her down. He seized the waistband of her skirt and she heard the material tear as she tried to scrabble away from him. He kicked her in the ribs and she felt the breath rush out of her in one gasp of searing pain as she tried to move, her fingers clawing at the carpet. But he was on top of her, pinning her down, too strong for her to resist. His sour breath sickened her and the horror reflected in his eyes stifled the scream swelling inside her chest. He had something in his hand and as she caught sight of it, saw it was a leather dog-collar. The scream was coming, but he grabbed her by the throat and cut it off. 'You want to be a bitch—' he spat the words into her face—'I'll show you how to be a bitch.'

'I thought you'd've brought a locksmith,' Bogan said to Harris in the passageway at Bosun's Reach. 'Don't tell me you're going to dirty those lilywhites and do it yourself.'

Harris ignored the jibe. He took a thin-bladed burglar's tool from the inside pocket of his Valentino. 'You don't need a locksmith for this crap,' he replied. 'I could spring this with a credit card, dead easy. You'd think they'd have more sense, the sort of money these pads cost, you'd think they'd fit a halfway decent lock instead of this junk.' He eased the blade into the lock, tickled the tangs and listened to the tumblers fall.

'Wish I'd been a detective,' Bogan said, arms folded, his shoulders against the wall, watching Harris work. 'With fancy tricks like that, I don't know why you don't join the Magic Circle, get yourself a blonde bimbo in fishnet tights and do the clubs on Saturday night. I bet you've got a couple of white rabbits tucked up your shirt.'

'You're too ugly for CID, pal,' Harris replied as he picked the lock with a flourish and the door swung open. 'Stick to persecuting motorists and leave the real job to the professionals.'

Bogan stepped into the lobby. 'I've nicked more villains than you've had hot dinners.' He kept up the banter. The carpet was sage green matching the Regency stripe of the wallpaper. Just inside the doorway there stood a small mahogany table with a white telephone on top.

'Oh yeah?' Harris followed him inside, looking around. 'What you get 'em for, spitting on the pavement?'

Bogan pushed open the sapele-veneered interior door which led into the living-room. 'All right, Michael Mitchell,' he muttered to himself, 'let's be having you.' Over his shoulder he said, 'Don't make me laugh, you lot couldn't detect shit if you trod in it.'

They stood just inside, looking down the L-shaped room towards the dining recess. An expensive Chinese rug stretched out before them, subtle pastel shades changing colour in the light from the picture window. A feather-filled Habitat settee, a big four-seater, sat against the wall opposite two matching easy chairs, all scattered with cushions in autumn shades and arranged to face a 24-inch colour TV squatting in a repro cabinet. The red eye of a video recorder glared balefully at them from its lair underneath the set. There were tables with lamps and the general effect was of a woman's touch, Bogan decided, all swanky pieces probably ordered from some fancy catalogue on monthly payment. All except the wetsuit thrown over the arm of one of the chairs. It was black with orange panels and looked out of place in this room.

'Not after you flatfoots have stomped all over it.' Harris wrinkled his nose. 'What's that smell?'

Bogan caught it at the same time, a sweet, sickly aroma. He shrugged, going after Harris again. 'So who'd our fink ask for when he called *Crimestoppers* on the Luxton robbery? Yours truly.' He tapped his chest as he examined the wetsuit as if Mitchell might be curled up inside. A knife scabbard strapped to the leg was empty.

'Well, I've got to give you that,' Harris conceded, abandoning the ribbing. 'We got chapter and verse on that one all right. Lunatic called Woodruff, Woody Woodruff, CRO as long as your arm . . . Hey, look at this.' As he spoke, he walked down to the dining area. 'Been a barney here all right.'

Bogan followed him. In the recess a whisky bottle lay in a pool of amber liquid which had seeped over the edge of a silver-plated drinks tray and had stained the top of the sideboard. A damask tablecloth had slipped from the top of an oval gateleg and lay crumpled on the carpet with cutlery strewn around. Crystal glasses and a decanter lay where they had fallen spilling puddles of red wine.

'Looks like a domestic.' Bogan sniffed, he was getting a bad feeling about the place, the smell strong in his nostrils, a half-familiar odour he didn't want to remember. Harris went over to the kitchen where the door was flung open. There were pots on the ceramic hob set into the onyx work surface, all the signs of a meal in preparation, but when he looked down at the tiled floor a puzzled expression formed on his face. Bogan joined him.

'So what d'you make of that, pal?' the DC asked, pointing to the bowl on the floor into which food had been slopped.

With the feeling of foreboding growing stronger Bogan said, 'Looks like some poor sod was in the doghouse.'

CHAPTER 17

Black wings enveloped her, dragged her down, and Jojo succumbed to the horror, too exhausted to struggle. The parrot had spoken, he was coming back to claim her. Her hand went to her neck and she could feel it even now, feel the dog-collar with its bright metal studs tighten around her throat.

Michael took the leather leash and clipped it on. When she tried to get up, he knocked her down again and began to drag her around on all fours, laughing and calling her a bitch. She skinned her knees as he hauled her into the kitchen and began slopping food from the pan into a bowl which he skittered across the floor. 'You want to eat? Get your nose in that, bitch,' he snarled, grabbing a fistful of her hair and pushing her down into the mess, plunging her face into the mash of sauce and eggplant. Jojo gagged and squirmed, but he wouldn't let up. 'Eat it, you dog!'

Jojo made lapping noises and Michael snapped the leash taut, cackling his drunken delight. Her eyes bulged and the once-familiar room blurred into an alien place as she was struck by the awful realization that he wouldn't let up. She was going to die. In front of her eyes, the Michael she knew had been transformed into some hideous creature bent on destroying her. He jerked her head back and peered at her, his bloated face swimming in and out of her vision. 'Oh, I get it . . . the bitch on heat.' The words oozed slime as he dragged her back into the living-room. 'Well, we can soon take care of that.'

Claws tearing at her underwear as she scuttled away from him on all fours, the collar choking her with each tug on the leash. He stood over her, fumbling with the belt on his trousers, distracted for a moment, and her frantic gaze fell on the wetsuit draped over the chair, the black handle of the knife filling her sight as she grabbed for it and the silver blade slid smoothly from the scabbard.

'Get your hands off me, you bastard!' She broke free and scrambled down the hall in blind panic. Anything to get away, but in her urgent haste she fled into the bedroom, and realized too late that she was trapped in a dead end.

Jojo staggered to her feet, numbed into an icy calm, the leather leash dangling from the collar around her neck. She held the knife in front of her and the blade seemed to stretch away forever. Michael lurched into the doorway, his trousers bunched ludicrously around his knees, his face twisted into a leer. He drifted towards her in slow motion, winding down into freeze frame. And the horror took possession of her, stiffened her muscles so that she would not flinch.

'You've got some lip on you, you know that,' Bogan said as they moved deeper into the flat. 'You want to watch your attitude or one fine day some big bastard with no sense of humour is going to fill you in.'

They were in the inner hall and Harris watched as Bogan opened a door on his left and looked inside. 'What I don't get is why you got the tip on the Luxton job. Why the voice asked for you. He was going to get the reward anyway.'

'You've got to put yourself about in this game,' Bogan replied, equally mystified, but with no intention of giving the cocky detective an inch. 'Sow enough seeds and you never know what'll come up sooner or later. The old art of coppering, you've got to work at it, get out on the street and put the fear of Christ into 'em. You young guys have got no idea.'

He stepped into the room and saw immediately that it served as an office. Harris was about to follow, but Bogan said, 'What d'you want to do, hold hands? I'll take this one, you have a look down there.' He gestured down the hall. 'You never know, you might strike lucky.'

'Yeah, and you might help yourself to his readies if I take my eye off you,' Harris said. 'I heard all about you old-time coppers.' Harris leaned against the doorjamb. 'If Mitchell starts squealing his nest-egg's vanished I might get the wrong idea about what you were up to in here. I'm your insurance, pal, and besides I like watching you work, might pick up some pointers.'

'Suit yourself,' Bogan said, taking in the room with a practised glance. There was a cheap kneehole desk under the window with a phone and fax machine on top. A couple of metal filing cabinets and a table strewn with catalogues and oddments of diving gear completed the spartan furnishings. Unlike the chintzy living-room, there was an untidy maleness about the den and he began to picture Michael Mitchell rummaging in the clutter of paperwork. Bogan went behind the desk and sat in the canvas-backed director's chair, getting the feel of the place. Red ink bills and final demands were strewn in front of him, ripped from their envelopes and tossed casually aside. He picked up a handful and glanced through them. The electricity and the phone were about to be cut off. Jack the Lad sitting there, his chickens coming home to roost. 'Look at this.' He showed them to Harris. 'This joker's going down for the third time. No wonder he's made himself scarce.'

'Probably off drumming up trade,' Harris said, 'bilking some other mugs.' He rifled through the pile of paper and whistled. 'He took this lot to the cleaners all right. Makes you wonder how he's got the brass neck to keep up the charade, he's in hock up to his ears. Look, he's using about a dozen different identities, there's enough here to do him for false pretences, conspiracy to defraud, theft, all sorts of misdemeanours, and that's just for starters.'

'He's been a naughty boy all right,' Bogan agreed. Looking through the desk drawer, he came across cheque-books and credit cards in the name of several different companies. He raised an eyebrow and showed them to Harris. 'Look at this little lot. He changes his name with his underpants.'

'Oh yeah,' Harris said. 'He's been kiting dud paper all over town. We'd better leave this to the Fraud Squad, pal. I've got a feeling they're going to want to take a close look at Mr Mitchell.'

'Not until I've finished with him,' Bogan said. He reached deeper into the drawer and came up with a wallet of snapshots which he spilled out on to the desk. He stirred the pictures with his finger until he found the one he was looking for. Lover-boy in his sailor suit giving the camera his big easy smile, his thick black hair slicked back, eyes set deep in a weatherbeaten face, the faint line of an old scar running down one cheek creating that hint of mystery. Bogan stared into the face of his quarry, recognizing the roguish tilt of the features as he committed them to memory. A chancer who lived on his wits. He slipped the snapshot into his pocket and got to his feet. 'Come on,' he told Harris, 'let's see what else our friend's got tucked away in here.'

They walked down the hall and Bogan poked his head into the bathroom. The bath was half filled with scummy water gone cold, the shower head dangling from the fitment, a fluffy blue towel draped over the washbowl. Took a bath, then took a powder, Bogan thought. Harris had his hand on the doorknob of the master bedroom. He turned the knob and applied a little pressure. The door began to swing open under his hand.

In the bedroom Michael closed on her, big and dangerous, and Jojo didn't stop to plead, didn't stop to think. She stuck him in a blind reflex and for a fleeting second was astonished how easily the knife went in, right up to the hilt. The razor sharp steel skewered the right ventricle and sent the cardiac muscle into spasm and Jojo heard her own voice shout 'Yes!' Just that single word. Michael stopped in his tracks and looked down in astonishment. Red seeped into the mustard polo shirt and he rocked back, the blade coming out in Jojo's hand in a fine spray of blood. A perplexed look filled Michael's eyes as he pulled up the shirt in disbelief and looked at the silly puncture as his ruptured heart pumped frantically and a geyser of blood exploded from the wound. His fingers clutched at the place, the bronzed muscles of his belly rippling in shock as the jet of bright red blood hosed the room. Eyes glazed and then refocused as he lunged forward with a grunt and grabbed Jojo by the throat, his bloodslicked fingers clamping on to her windpipe so tight that her head swam. Desperately she raised the knife and plunged it into him again just below the neck, finding it harder this time as the blade jarred off the collar-bone before slicing into a lung. 'Yes!' Jojo cried tearing herself free, breathing hard, 'Oh yes!'

Pink froth bubbled from his mouth as he came at her again, swinging an arm which swept her aside, casual as swatting a fly. She fell on to the bed and he grabbed at the knife, clutching the blade. She wrenched it loose and saw bone where the razor steel had all but severed his fingers. But still he didn't stop. She scampered across the duvet and crouched in the narrow gap between the far side of the bed and the wall, holding the bloody knife out in front of her, her lips pulled back in a snarl. Michael swayed for a moment, befuddled, and then summoned up his remaining strength. 'Jojo!' Her name gurgled in his throat as he drove forward, and he would have been upon her again but for the moleskin slacks which had slipped from his knees to around his ankles and hobbled him. His balance gone, Michael sprawled headlong on the carpet and she sprang at him, trailing the dog-leash, and plunged the knife repeatedly into his back above the black silk boxer shorts. 'Yes . . . yes . . . yes!' Her voice rose with each stab. Ten, twenty times the blade arced down. 'Yes . . . oh yes!' Her voice rose to a scream as she straddled him, hacking at his flesh until her strength was spent, and she fell to one side, curled up against the pleats of the divan cover and began to whimper.

She lay there for what seemed an eternity, letting the tension drain out of her, expecting to wake from a nightmare. She opened her eyes. Michael was lying beside her. In trepidation she reached out and prodded his shoulder. He didn't move.

Bogan pulled his head out of the bathroom and looked for Harris who had gone through the door into the master bedroom. He was about to follow when the detective reappeared suddenly, his face deathly white, sweat beading his upper lip. He swayed against the door and seemed about to faint and Bogan felt the hairs rising on his own neck as his expression asked the question. Harris stared at him, eyes wide in shock, groping for the words. 'Jesus,' he breathed, 'Jesus Christ . . . it's like an abattoir in there.'

Blood filled her eyes. As reality edged back in, Jojo slowly realized that she was standing there, barefoot, in nothing more than her white cotton panties, shuddering from shock, the knife still clutched in her hand.

Her eyes took in the bedroom on which she had lavished so much care, the candy-striped duvet cover, the pastel walls, the full drape of the pretty Laura Ashley prints which curtained the window, gathered up in gold tassels. Such an intimate nest in which they had loved each other, where she and Michael had lain together like spoons in a drawer and shared each other's dreams.

Now there was just blood, her fripperies draped in blood as though some manic hand had aerosoled the room. Her special place desecrated, part of her torn out by this bloody pulp stretched full length at her feet, this carcase wallowing in its own gore. She wanted the thing out of there, and she grabbed the blood sodden shirt and tried to pull it across the floor, but it was too heavy for her, a dead weight. The swimming moody madness seeped back into her. Michael, her Michael was gone. All that was left was the thing with its thick bare legs entwined in the moleskin slacks. Agitation danced like an itch she couldn't reach. Get it out of here, screamed her inner voice, get it out of my bedroom, my special place where I slept in Michael's arms and we were happy. Look at it, leaking its thick red goo, it was too obscene!

The images fragmented, blurred, came together again as she heaved at the carcass, but still couldn't move it. One image stood out from the whirling picture show inside her head, a sliver of memory, a snatched glimpse into the back room of a butcher's shop where she went as a little girl; beyond the high counter with its white slabs, a glimpse through the swing door into the back, catching sight of the red-stained block where the skinned animals were butchered, the door swinging shut, cutting off the dreadful sight, etching it into her memory. Jojo straightened, gasping from the exertion. She told herself she had to get the thing out of there before Michael came back. My God, he might walk in any minute! She was going frantic when her eyes fell on the diver's knife in her hand and very slowly she turned the blade over and examined the serrated edge, the fine teeth keen enough to saw through a hawser. And the lens of her feverish mind recaptured the picture, froze the frame . . . a glimpse into the butcher's shop.

Bogan looked into the bedroom from the doorway and fought back the urge to get out of there, to turn away before the scene became imprinted on his retina and joined the catalogue of sights which bad dreams were made of. He could hear Harris beside him, his breath rasping as he wrestled with his own devil. Immediately in front of him

Bogan saw that the white shag pile was matted in a puddle of thick viscous blood which had dried into a rusty crust. Red splashes radiated out, stark against the carpet. The duvet flung over the king-sized Habitat bed was drenched and whorls and loops disfigured the walls like surrealist art. Even the artexed ceiling with its biscuit-shaded tulip lightshade was spattered red. Released from the close confines of the room, the sweet, sickly stench turned his stomach.

Harris said, 'Mitchell?'

'Well, it sure as hell isn't a heavy nosebleed,' Bogan replied, disguising his queasiness with heavy sarcasm.

'Jesus, I've seen some things.' Harris stared, moisture slicking his upper lip. 'But I swear I never saw anything like that before.' His voice was tinged with awe. 'How could anybody bleed that much and walk away? It's not possible.'

'Well, this poor bastard did,' Bogan said, checking the room over. His eyes alighted on the louvred doors of the fitted wardrobe and he felt a sensation like a spring tightening in his chest.

Harris followed his gaze. There was nowhere else to hide, nowhere else to crawl away. 'You want to take a look?' he asked.

Bogan looked at him and his lip curled. 'What's the matter, you chicken?'

The muscles bunched along Harris's jaw as his stomach revolted and his forehead turned greasy. 'I just thought . . . we ought to leave it, get some back-up out here.'

'And look like prize prats if we didn't turn up something, right under our noses?' The words thickened in Bogan's throat as he staved off his revulsion, imagining what he might find. He sucked in a deep breath, his own stubborn determination to score one off the smart-alec detective willing his legs to move. He edged cautiously around the bedroom, his heart cannoning off his ribs, reached out to the gilt knob and gingerly slid the wardrobe door open, fighting the urge to flinch back. A neat rack of clothes, suits one end, dresses the other, appeared in the recess. He parted them with his fingers. There was nothing more sinister than an assortment of shoes.

Bogan turned, a gleam of triumph in his eyes. 'Clean as a whistle,' he told Harris. 'Let's give 'em a bell, there's nobody here.'

They went back into the den, careful now not to disturb anything. Whatever had happened here, the flat had now become a crime scene to be painstakingly searched by the men in disposable paper overalls. Whatever frenzied violence had brutalized the place, it was no longer their problem. They were just the foot soldiers, the tumbling clowns, waiting to hand over the show to the ringmaster. But it didn't stop them speculating.

'The way he was carrying on, he must've made plenty of enemies,' Harris said. 'Maybe one of them came round to give him a good hiding.'

'Yeah? And then they kissed and made up and went out for a takeaway?' Bogan shook his head. 'More likely our Michael did the pasting, then took off.'

Harris said, 'Couldn't have happened. Bleed like that, you're not going to get out the door, and there's no blood anywhere else.'

'OK, genius,' Bogan said. 'Where'd he go, down the plughole? There's nobody here.'

Harris thought about it for a moment and then he shrugged his shoulders. 'You've got me there, pal,' he had to admit.

As they knocked down each other's theories, Bogan became restless to be gone. He began to pace the room, examining his uniform, brushing off flecks of dust, picking at specks of lint, pinching the crease in his trousers with thumb and forefinger, anything to keep his mind off the scene in the adjacent room. Riddles unnerved him, not that he cared overmuch. All he had to do was sit there and wait for the CID to arrive. They got paid to unravel riddles, but all the same he felt an overwhelming urge to put the job out of his mind for an hour or two and unwind over a beer and a few laughs.

'What about his bird, our little Jojo?' Harris said. 'Where's she fit into the picture?'

'Buggered if I know,' Bogan said, his thought returning to the bridge. 'Probably came home, saw the mess and flipped.' He pictured the tiny turquoise butterfly, high on the steel.

'So what about your mate? He must've been nuts to go up there on his tod.'

Bogan thought about Nigel. That was something else he didn't care to contemplate now that he knew he could do nothing more for the negotiator. That stuck-up bird still worrying away at his memory was just going to have to busk it.

'Silly sod wouldn't listen to reason,' he began to justify himself, almost believing it. 'I told him not to, but he wouldn't see sense. Started giving me all that crap about duty. Turned my back and he was off like a long dog.' He shook his head. 'Send off the packet tops and get a fancy degree, think they know it all. Kids we're getting in the job wouldn't have passed muster in my day.'

When they ran out of small talk, Harris relented from his chaperone duty on the understanding that his squeamishness would not figure in any canteen jokes and stepped out for a breath of fresh air. Alone in the den, Bogan sat down at the desk and stared at the phone. What the hell, he thought, as he snatched it up and tapped in Iris's number, it was worth one last try. The phone rang and rang without reply. Bogan put it down, the ache in his loins ruling his head. He picked it up again and rang Maddie at home, taking a risk the double-glazing king might answer. Her voice came on the line.

'Can you get away tonight?' he asked her, throwing caution to the wind.

She gurgled deep in her throat and he imagined those blancmange breasts trembling deliciously. 'Charlie saw you on the TV, on the news. He's mad as a nit you got more exposure than he did with his crummy commercial, now he's sulking, the little creep.' She paused. 'I thought you said we were going to cool it?'

'I can't resist you,' Bogan said. 'You know you're my first mate, sweetheart. Can you get down to the boat?' He lifted a boot up the desk to check the spit shine.

'You only have to say the word, Teddy—' her voice intimate—'and I come running. You know what you do to me.'

'I'll be there as soon as I can get away,' Bogan said. 'Don't wait up.'

She giggled. 'Coxswain coming aboard. I'll be waiting. Oh, and by the way, I thought you looked really hunky on TV. I could eat you.'

Bogan put the phone down, peered at his reflection in the toecap of his Doc. He was feeling better already, his ego restored. What a romeo, he thought, what a player. He lowered the gleaming boot to the floor and as he did so he knocked one of the papers from the pile scattered on the desktop. It fluttered down, two pages of official-looking document stapled together. Bogan reached over, picked it up and took a look. It was a photocopy of a court order giving judgement to the finance house to repossess one Jaguar XJS convertible, colour yellow.

CHAPTER 18

Up on Ecstasy, the Wharf Rats swaggered into the multi-storey. There were three of them, kids from the street gang which held sway in the rundown neighbourhood, preening themselves in their sweatshirts and faded jeans slashed at the knee, throwing playful punches, kicking out their huge air-sole Reeboks, carefully unlaced so that the tongues flapped as they jigged and bounced. The trio were the coolest of the cool, chilled out, popping E, ready for action. Not one of them was a day over fifteen, yet under the slicked-back hair their acne-ravaged faces were worldly wise.

They danced around an old Ford transit parked on the lower deck and when the cab doors refused to budge, vented their spleen by giving the van a good kicking. They pranced up the ramp to the second level and gave a rusty Datsun and an ancient Allegro the same treatment. A bronze Sierra with a buckled wing proved more fruitful, but although they could get inside and bounce around on the seats, the complexities of hot-wiring the ignition proved beyond them and they demonstrated their disgust by throwing open all the doors and urinating into the car, taking bets on who could pee the furthest.

Gleefully, the Wharf Rats bounded up to the third floor and through the gloom immediately spotted the yellow XJS. They approached the car with goggling reverence, circled it with exaggerated caution, exchanging glances as if they had stumbled upon some life-form from another planet. The boldest of them, his larded hair scraped back from a pimply forehead, peered in at the driver's window. His hand explored the sleek sweep of the coachwork and his fingers tried the recessed catch. The unlocked door clicked and swung open. Keys dangled temptingly from the ignition.

They looked at each other, eyes popping, unable to believe their luck, and then, whooping with delight, fell upon the Jaguar. Pimples was behind the wheel. He turned the key, his foot flat down and the engine roared into life. The others slapped him about the head as he worked the T-bar and the XJS slewed out of the slot, tyres smoking. He yanked on the handbrake just to get the feel of it. Oh yeah, now they'd really show those Eastgate dickheads with their crappy wheels a thing or two. Burn the bastards off!

Fifteen minutes later, an unmarked white Escort SOCO van came down the dock road, turned into the multi-storey car park and traversed the ramps to the third level. Two men in polyester suits got out and looked around. Inside the van a police radio droned monotonously. 'Typical,' the older of the two told his partner, disgust on his face, 'we bust a gut to get over here, and what do they do . . . send us to the wrong place.'

Afterwards Jojo ran the bath as hot as she could stand it. She poured in strawberry salts and slipped into the water, immersing herself in the rich foam until she was sure the muck was washed away. Lay there, her body idling, until the water first turned tepid and then chilly. She got out of the bath and dried herself vigorously, making her skin glow, tied her hair back in a ponytail, put on her towelling robe and padded into the living-room where she curled up on the settee, picked up the remote and turned on the TV, hopping channels until she settled for the night movie, some American courtroom drama where everybody seemed to turn to the screen and make a speech. It was part way through and she couldn't follow the plot, but the drone of the voices soothed her and she fell asleep.

Jojo opened her eyes. The clock on the mantel said six o'clock and the bright light of morning was already streaming through the window. Some slapstick breakfast show was starting on the TV and she switched it off, and in the heavy silence punctuated only by the ticking of the central heating, she strolled into the bathroom, took off her robe and went through her usual morning routine, then took her turquoise shell suit from the airing cupboard and put it on. Frowning slightly in concentration, she sorted through the contents of her handbag, put on her white doeskin kickers and left the flat. The front door clicked shut behind her.

Jojo went down to the underground garage where the Jaguar was parked, got into the car and drove out of Bosun's Reach. There was a tape already in the cassette slot and when she pressed the button, The Doors blasted a rock beat into the car.

It came back to her, on the bridge, in the gathering twilight, every move she'd made laid out for close examination. She was diving down, deep into herself, striking out for the dark place where the memories couldn't follow. The chattering parrot in her lap no longer bothered her. It kept on talking, but she wasn't listening any more. The spangle of the city was just a faraway blur in the thickening mist, fading into absolute darkness. Wearily she became annoyed with herself, leaving it this late to follow Michael, scolding herself that if she dallied longer he would be too far ahead and she would have no chance of catching up. It was time, but she had one thing left to do. She would keep her promise to this poor creature clinging to her, handcuff his arms around the girder so that he couldn't fall. 'Come on, my love,' she whispered in his ear, 'no time for this foolishness now, time to say goodbye.'

'Post Traumatic Stress Disorder, that's what the doc says,' Vicky told Bert Royal. Her face was drained, washed out, her cheeks blotchy, the lines etched from the side of her nose to the corners of her mouth pulling her expression down. 'Must've triggered something from the past—' she massaged her brow with fingers and thumb—'something we don't know a damned thing about.'

Royal looked across at the psychologist they'd called in to help, a lanky young man with a shock of curly dark hair. He seemed bemused, lost in his own thoughts, disorientated by the activity inside the command truck. He returned to Vicky, watching her age as she burned herself out trying to get through to the couple perched high above them. The diagnosis on Nigel Wilcox stunned him. 'What's that mean?' he asked.

Vicky sighed. 'Basically he's not functioning any more, and there's no way we're going to be able to get through to him. Whatever happened up there has thrown his mind into neutral, he just can't hack it.'

Royal stared at her in disbelief. The woman who called herself Jojo, he could understand. Some event had tipped her over the edge, that was obvious, but Wilcox? Was it possible that they had missed some gaping flaw in his character. He pictured the kid around the station, keen as mustard, eager to please. One of the new breed from the universities so assiduously wooed into the force to give the job a veneer of brainpower. Could he really have just blown a fuse?'

Shaking his head, Royal said, 'Keep after the woman, Vicky, keep her talking.' He rested a hand on the shoulder of Jack Rivers's daughter. 'You're doing a great job, Inspector, just concentrate on Jojo. The lads are almost in position. It's all over bar the shouting.'

Vicky looked puzzled, her eyes pained. 'Dammit, I must've missed something,' she berated herself. 'Should've tried harder . . .'

'Stop that,' Royal told her gruffly, 'you're twice as good as any man, remember? You don't have to prove a thing, least of all to me.'

He squeezed her shoulder and she looked up at him and

was about to speak when Davies appeared at the door and told them, 'We're ready up top.'

Trained low, the searchlights on the bridge stabbed into the murk rising from the river, hardly penetrating the shroud which enveloped the superstructure where the Task Force teams, lashed in safety harnesses, groped their way down the long sweep of the cable at a heart-skipping snail's pace. Despite its tree-trunk girth, the cable swayed and grunted and at times they became so disorientated they had to halt their descent to allow jangled nerves to settle. After what seemed an eternity, one team reached a spot from which they could just make out the outline of their quarry huddled on the web of girders directly below.

They sent the silent signal to stop all movement, two clicks of the transmit button on the open channel, and with hand signals only, began to rope up ready to abseil down. They huddled, faces slicked from the wet drizzle, tested the nylon rope against the shackles, tugged against the stainless steel friction clips one last time, and then the team leader, eyes straining, raised his hand in front of their faces. Muscles tensed. When the hand dropped they would go for it.

Nigel Wilcox snapped out of it as Jojo untwined herself from his grasp, took hold of his hands and said, 'Come on, lovey, it's time. Put your arms around it, look, it's easy. You're going to be all right.'

But Nigel couldn't make out the words. His eyes opened so wide that his cheeks went taut and his forehead wrinkled. He came out of the trance so abruptly that the shock to his system left him dazed. What the hell! Everything was blurry, and all he could really make out as his pupils dilated was that he was on some sort of foggy perch, his arms outstretched, a woman somehow familiar at his side, clutching at his hands.

Jesus! His face flushed as he realized he must have blacked out and a flash flood of adrenalin twitched his dormant muscles back into life and in the same instant, Nigel felt his brain swelling inside his skull, about to explode. Do something! his voice shrilled inside his head, sending an overload into his limbs. Twitching like a marionette, he snatched free, leaped to his feet, saw the woman's face floating in the murk, just a pale oval, eyes huge. So maddeningly familiar, he ached to shout out, but her name was gone. What the hell was her name? His memory cartwheeled back into his worst nightmare, back to his alma mater, clinging to the brickwork of the old tower, paralysed with fright. That moment of shame. Sweet Jesus! Toes clenched inside his boots as he swayed on the girder. Half turned, reached for the woman, desperate to remember.

Jojo was caught off guard. The parrot distracted her as down below in the command truck Vicky Rivers summoned the last throw of feminine intuition. 'Michael hurt you, didn't he, Jojo?' It was worth a try, there was nothing to lose. 'Listen . . . listen to me . . .' holding her breath so that the tension inside her wouldn't show. 'We've got him now, he's confessed!' injecting a lift of optimism into her voice. 'We'll put him away, he won't ever hurt you again.' Thank God . . . Jojo felt a warm rush of relief. The leaden weight was lifted, it was out of her hands. She went to squeeze the button, tell the voice it was over, when the parrot flew out of her hand squawking and dancing on its wire as Nigel squirmed from her grasp and sprang up like a gymnast on the bar. 'No,' she yelped, reeling. 'Don't!' and glimpsed his face suddenly animated under the shock of ginger hair as he turned towards her, uncomprehending. She clung to the girder to stop herself from falling. 'Nigel . . . no!' Her voice was frantic as his head snapped away and she freed one hand, lunged for the belt of his tunic, grabbed a handful of cloth, held him tight.

Nigel spotted the movement out of the corner of his eye, black shapes materializing out of the gloaming. Jojo saw them in the same instant, swinging out of nowhere. Everything happening at once, too much to take in. Suddenly she felt hollow as a husk, as if her insides had been scooped out and strung on the iron, strips of entrail, bloody tissue. Like the punchline of a sick joke, that sweet voice of reason had betrayed her! Dancing in front of her she saw the twist. Michael's face! The joke was on her. 'No!' she heard herself scream as she tripped out and went numb.

Nigel heard the scream close by, but it didn't register as his mind spun in a frantic whirl. Shapes materialized out of the fog, lunged at him calling words he couldn't make out.

Searchlights stabbed up through the drenching mist as Jojo jumped. Stretched on to her toes and the soles of her kickers left the girder in a little hop. Releasing Nigel's tunic, she jumped for the dazzling white eye glaring up at her and was already on her way down when hands grabbed her shell suit and hauled her back. The Michael masks vanished! Faces she didn't recognize frozen rigid, mouthed words she couldn't hear over the roaring in her ears as they fettered her arms and legs, squeezing the breath out of her. The second team swarmed down and they grabbed her, yelling at her not to struggle; she was safe, it was all over. But Jojo squirmed in the straitjacket, trying to get a look over their bunched shoulders. Her eyes strained in their sockets. Where was he?

Nigel teetered in the mist as the figures closed around him, clutching at him. Instinctively he flinched back and lost his precarious balance. Blank astonishment wiped out all sensation as his feet found no resistance, and he hung suspended for a second, as he tried to grab the outstretched hands, fingers slipping. In a surge of fright, clarity struck him like a blow to the forehead. Bogan. The woman. He was on the bridge! Reeling from the shock to his nervous system, sinew and muscle abandoned the struggle, went limp as the suffocating folds of sea fog enveloped him and he slid from their grasp. Plunging like a stone, blood roaring in his ears, his arms flailing the soft formless carpet which bore him down, that last elusive fragment of memory clicked into place. Her face filled his mind with an anguish so real it ripped his heart. The scream burst from his gaping mouth.

'Jojo!'

CHAPTER 19

Vicky Rivers heard the scream on her headphones. She pulled them off and cast them aside, unable to bear the cry which split her head. In front of her the scanner went crazy, numbers skipping across the display as the electronics tried to recapture the lost frequency. Vicky watched the flashing numerals in a daze and then, with a supreme effort, reached down and lifted her handbag on to her lap, took out her compact, opened it, and reviewed her face in the mirror. She applied make-up, a touch of lipstick, brushed her hair, dabbed a little *Je Reviens* behind the lobes of her ears and on the inside of her wrists, and rebuilt her composure as anguish writhed within her, pleading to escape. She fought not to admit her weakness, until finally she reached out and cut the power. The numbers stopped flashing and the tape ran down. She became conscious of the brooding silence which had supplanted the clamour inside the command truck, the only sound the steady hum of the generator as the crew fell silent, exchanging embarrassed glances, nothing left to do. When she could stand it no longer, Vicky got to her feet, smoothed her skirt, and moved to the door. Cool and professional. Show no emotion.

Stepping from the cocoon of her artificial world, she was surprised by the mist which had thickened into drizzle throwing ghostly haloes around the bridge lights. She shivered in the chill air and then walked stiffly across the greasy wet asphalt to where Bert Royal was leaning over the rail, peering down into the murk, Davies beside him, radio in hand, talking to the Ministry of Defence police launch searching the river below. She heard Royal say: 'What's the use, they've got no chance, bitch of a current's running like a train, going to take him out past Crab Point and feed him to the fishes. Poor devil's going to be picked clean before we get him back.' His pink bald pate shone wet as he straightened and looked at her, distracted, taking a moment for her face to register, an awkward speechless moment as he dredged for some comforting words. Oh, not the barrack-room exchanges they used to hide their grief, not for little Vicky, the interloper in her pert suit and her high heels. Syrup for her, a patronizing pat on the head, tell her she was a good girl, she'd done her best. She could read it on his battered, anguished face and prickled with hostility.

'Welcome to the freak show.' She gave him a slow handclap. 'Scored high on artistic impression, so who cares if it all went to rats.' She arched an eyebrow. 'Got to look good for the media. What're you going to tell 'em? Hero cop saves the lady, takes the dive?'

Vicky raised a hand and pointed to where the Task Force men were bringing Jojo down from the tower, carrying her to the waiting ambulance, its doors open, throwing a fuzzy glare into the mist. Royal turned just in time to see the paramedics fussing over a glimpse of turquoise, wrapping the small limp figure in red thermal blankets, lifting her into the blur of light, the shadows suddenly popping with flashguns, the flare of TV lights as cameramen rushed up, cursing and jostling as they thrust their lenses into the opening. Like a scene from bedlam.

'You'll pardon me, sir, if I don't stay for your act,' Vicky said, anxious to escape the madhouse before her brittle resolve cracked. 'Don't think my stomach could stand it. Besides, I've got work to do, so I'll see you back at the nick. We've got some unfinished business, remember?' Hitting him where it hurt.

Royal swung back to her as the ambulance moved off with a whirr of its siren. But not before one of the newsmen had spotted him and with a whoop the hunting pack bore down on its next victim. He caught the arrogant defiance in Vicky's eyes and in that instant Royal was consumed with an overwhelming urge to lay his hand across her face, to shake the mule-stubborn stupidity out of her. Vicky Rivers, toughing it out, aping a father she never really knew. He wanted to give it to her right there and then, tell her just how tarnished the legend really was. Do it for her own good, before it was too late. The words were on his lips when the first microphone was thrust into his face and the TV lights came on, dazzling him. Instead Bert Royal bit his tongue and fished out his car keys, handed them to Vicky. 'Take my car, Inspector,' he told her. 'I'll get a ride back when I've finished here.'

Bogan was sitting in the Incident Car, hands resting on the wheel, just staring through the windscreen, when Royal found him and got in on the passenger's side.

'You all right?'

'I'll live.' Bogan looked at him.

Royal sank back in the seat, his head against the rest. 'You know I didn't have a choice.' He met the accusing embers of the other's eyes. 'Headquarters was watching it go from bad to worse on the TV. It was shot to shingles. We had to do something. They just wanted it off the box, before the politicians got in on the act. Over and done with, end of story.'

He massaged his forehead. 'Who would've believed it could've gone like that. The guys on the bridge were all set, visibility was going down.' He sighed heavily. 'What with Wilcox not responding and the woman psyching herself up to jump, I had to give the word. Go in fast.'

Bogan washed his hand over his cheeks and pinched the bridge of his nose. He looked exhausted, emotionally drained. Royal said, 'If I hadn't done it, gold would have. What else could we do? Our guys swinging up there with their arses out to dry, naturally they went for the woman.

I mean, Jesus, nobody expected a cop to just step off like that.'

Bogan's head wagged from side to side. 'It should never have happened . . .'

'You're right, it shouldn't,' Royal agreed. 'If you'd've found her boyfriend, maybe we could have bought some more time. What the hell was that all about?'

'Christ only knows,' Bogan said. He'd left Harris at Bosun's Reach when the CID had arrived and had hurried back to the Arrow Bridge. 'We walked into a bloodbath. If you ask me, he took off like a scalded cat. How about the woman, she throw any light on it?'

'She's in shock,' Royal said. 'They took her to St Philip's, and we've put a WPC at her bedside. Bloodbath?' He looked puzzled. 'None of this makes sense.'

They were clearing the bridge, packing up and going home. Under the arc lamps uniformed figures moved about loading emergency equipment back into the trucks, stacking cones and dismantling the barricades. The crowd had drifted away, the drama over, and a couple of motor patrolmen in reflective jackets were waving traffic through the tolls in a desultory manner. It was free ride night across the Arrow Bridge.

'You shouldn've let me talk to him, gaffer,' Bogan said without rancour. Like all street cops, he was a pragmatist. Once it was over, that was it, no inquests, no recriminations. 'Maybe I could've got through to him.'

'And gold would've fried me,' Royal said. 'You know the rules: only trained negotiators do the talking.'

'So who was the lady on the horn? She looked familiar, but I'm damned if I could place her.'

Royal said, 'Jack Rivers's daughter.' Watched it dawn on Bogan's face. 'Vicky Rivers. Would you believe it, she's an inspector in Complaints and Discipline.'

'Jack Rivers's kid a rubber heel?' Bogan laughed shortly.'That takes some beating. I worked with him once, you know, gaffer, way back when I was an aide, carried his bags on a couple of jobs. It was an education all right, opened my eyes. Old Jack the magician. Boy, I wanted some of that CID glory in those days, wanted it so bad it hurt.'

'What happened?' Royal asked.

Bogan shrugged. 'First I got married, then I put a few noses out of joint, got the wrong side of a DI on the squad. They kicked me back to the blue suits.'

Royal rubbed his eyes, suddenly weary. 'It figures,' he said. 'In those days CID were cock of the walk.'

'You know the trouble with this job,' Bogan said. 'There's no characters any more. It's got boring.'

'There's still you and me,' Royal said. 'Last of the breed.'

'Yeah, but it's getting lonely out there.'

'You thought about putting your ticket in, Ted?'

'Long and hard, gaffer. Might just do it too, pull the pin.' He shrugged. 'Only what the hell else'd I be any good for, an old thief-taker like me?' A thought struck him and he gave Royal a sharp glance. 'Complaints and Discipline. What's a rubber heel doing on our patch?'

Royal looked away. Now was the moment of truth. Vicky would be back at the station waiting to pounce, and all those years pounding the pavement would count for nothing. Up against Jack Rivers's daughter, Bogan didn't stand a chance. He'd go like a lamb to the slaughter; required to resign as an alternative to dismissal. That was the formula. A kangaroo court in front of the chief and he'd be out on his ear. No pension, no nothing. Clear your locker, hand in the warrant card and the uniform and take a walk. Once Vicky got her claws into him, all that street savvy, all those bullshit years, would count for nothing. Bogan wouldn't have a prayer.

'She was the on-call negotiator,' Royal replied, ducking the question of loyalty. 'Did a pretty good job too.'

'Didn't save him though, did she? Love of Christ, he was

my crewmate!' Bogan's eyes were red-rimmed and his lip trembled.

Royal pulled himself up in the seat, embarrassed at the outburst of emotion. 'We're just about finished here,' he said. 'Get going, you can drive me back to the nick.'

'Sorry, gaffer.' Bogan sniffed as he started the engine. 'Don't know what came over me.' He swung the Montego around on the bridge approach and headed up town. The remnants of the rush hour had cleared, and there was a lull on the streets as the city took a breather before the tide turned and the revellers came pouring in, filling the pubs and the clubs. Under orange neon, colour leaked into the mist, leaving only a dreary monochrome to paint the concrete canyons. Each occupied with his own thoughts, they rode in silence, and the only sound in the car came from the police radio chattering between them.

The sands were running out. They had almost made it back to the station when Royal heard it, the ten code breaking through the routine exchanges to summon all available units. The Superintendent came upright in his seat. Rioting had broken out on the Eastgate estate and gangs of youths were on the rampage, stoning the police. Officers responding were being driven back by a hail of petrol bombs. 'That's all we need,' he groaned, almost glad of the diversion. 'Bloody Eastgate's exploded again. We'd better get over there.'

Unaware of Royal's dilemma, Bogan hesitated. He could see the police station up ahead, the lights inviting. 'Oh, have a heart, gaffer,' he protested, 'the shift's over. Haven't we had enough for one day?'

Royal gave him a hard glance. 'You want to see another Nigel Wilcox get his stupid head broken? Get a move on.'

Heaving on the wheel, Bogan's thoughts turned to Maddie waiting for him on the boat, and he felt like slamming on the brakes, ripping off the uniform and walking away. Stuff the job. But when he saw his own face reflected in the driving mirror he couldn't do it and, muttering an oath under his breath, he swung the Montego through a U-turn, hit the lights and the siren and jammed his foot down.

CHAPTER 20

The yellow XJS convertible hit the strip with the speedo touching eighty. Inside the Jaguar the two passengers bounced on the seats and egged the driver on. The Wharf Rats were coming, the Ecstasy gladiators. Now those Eastgate posers would see a thing or two!

As the sleek sportster burst into view the crowd roared approval. This was the best yet. Some chilled dudes had nicked a Jag from millionaires' row. Hot shit!

The XJS topped the ton on the straight, holding the line. The driver ratcheted the lever between the front seats, and the Jaguar slewed into a handbrake turn, smoking rubber. The mob erupted in delight. He trod the pedal and the yellow Jag leaped forward, pinning him back in the seat as the needles wound around in front of his eyes, and he swung the wheel and jerked the brake on again, locking up into another spectacular skid. The big cat hunkered down, rocking wildly on its suspension, taking the punishment like a thoroughbred.

High on E, the trio hung out of the windows yelling, 'Wharf Rats rule!' Then the pimpled wheelman, the driver-of-the-night award already within his grasp, spun the power steering and gunned the Jag into an encore. This time he hit a hundred and ten before he reached for the brake, and in the slam of deceleration felt a stab of pain in his calf. With a yelp he let go the lever and looked down in alarm. A knife catapulted from under his seat was sticking in his leg. A squeal of panic burst from his lips and his hands released the wheel.

Not even the race-bred Jaguar could cope with a tailspin at that speed. The rear end broke away and the XJS yawed out of control. The driver jerked up, saw the blur of faces through the windscreen as he tried to grab the spinning steering-wheel, but he was already rising out of his seat as the Jag left the road, leaped a bank and plunged down the other side. His head pushed hard against the lining of the hood, the wheel suddenly beyond his grasp as the big cat took over, running blind from her tormentors. For a split second he saw the windscreen rush towards him, shatter into a million fragments, filling his eyes. So quick, he couldn't work it out. He wondered what was happening. He wondered where the knife had come from. He wondered . . .

The skirmishing had begun in earnest when Bert Royal and Bogan arrived. In one brief and violent encounter the riot squad had baton-charged the mob and the troglodytes had scurried back to the safety of the drab towers to yell taunts and throw beer cans from the balconies as the police vans, grilles down, circled warily around. But the retreat was just a ploy to lure the battle waggons deeper into the estate, and once there, the Eastgate guerrillas, well versed in urban warfare, grabbed their makeshift weapons, reformed their battalions and counter-charged. Cut off from their line of retreat, the PSUs squealed for reinforcements as they fought a desperate rearguard action.

Smoke from burning barricades drifted across the estate, thickening the mist into a sooty smog. Figures flitted through the haze as fire and ambulance crews moved in behind the blue ranks, ready to mop up the misery.

PSU formations crouched behind their plastic shields under a hail of rocks and molotov cocktails, the snatch squads darting out, batons swinging to engage the leading ranks of the mob in hand to hand combat. In the orange blur, the black cliffs of the tower blocks loomed like fortresses over a scene of medieval battle.

At Royal's insistence, Bogan drove around the estate, his

right foot poised to floor the accelerator if they ran into trouble. But his reflexes were not quick enough when, out of nowhere, the whooping mob materialized in the headlights and began to stone the police car. Bogan snatched the gear-lever into reverse and was backing up when a hooded figure wielding a scaffolding pole dashed from the shadows and speared the rear window, spraying the interior with fragments of glass.

'Jesus!' Bogan yelped as he slewed the car around. 'Let's get out of here! I didn't join to take this shit.'

Also shaken by the display of raw violence, Bert Royal gritted his teeth and fought back the instinct to flee. It was his sub-division, his command, and he couldn't abandon his lads. Once they were out of immediate danger, he ordered Bogan to pull over and, shielding his eyes against the flickering glare, spotted a group from one of the Transits huddled over a fallen figure. When Bogan stopped the Montego close by, Royal forced himself to get out, debris crunching under his shoes. He went over to the group, swaddled in their flameproof overalls, the visors of their blue Nato helmets pushed up, saw bewilderment on their schoolboy faces. The man on the ground wore the sergeant's stripes of the team leader and was bleeding from a head wound, his eyes rolling in his head. The group parted as Royal came up, stared at him blankly out of gaunt, shocked faces. Jesus, he cursed bitterly, suddenly old as Methuselah, why was it always just kids!

He turned away so that they wouldn't see how badly his hands were trembling. Bogan was right, they didn't join up to fight bloody pitched battles on the streets. God, how he yearned for the old days, when the lines were clearly drawn, when they pitted their wits against villains who knew the score and stood still for a conviction instead of running screaming to the Court of Appeal. When the uniform meant something. When the gutters weren't red with blood. When

Jack Rivers had run the CID from the back bars of countless neighbourhood pubs.

He thought of Vicky then, waiting back at the station to crucify one of their own just to live up to her old man's reputation as a crackerjack investigator. Could he destroy her with the truth? Sit her down and tell her the secret which had bubbled up from the murky depths of his memory when he saw the old man in her eyes; that Jack Rivers, the great CID chief, had been just as corrupt, living by the booze and the bung; that every stick of furniture in the home she'd been brought up in, every bag of grocery, every toy she'd played with, had been acquired on the arm, free gratis, a favour in kind? His head sagged. It was the fraternal bond he and Jack had shared, but how could he make her understand that in those days, when the pay was poor and the hours long, conduct which would now be branded as corruption had carried no such stigma. It had simply been their way of life in those simple times before joyriders sparked senseless riots which tore the heart out of his town; before kids in police uniforms bled into the mud.

He rubbed his eyes, smarting from the acrid smoke. No, he couldn't bring himself to do it. There was only one other way out in which the honour of the cloth could be preserved, and he would have to cauterize the wound now, before his resolve evaporated. Tell Ted Bogan his fortune: that the rubber heels were on to his little game, that touch of enterprise which Jack Rivers would have so applauded. Tell him straight that he wanted his resignation on his desk by morning so that he could at least save him from the ignominy of a discipline, convince him by laying bare his own soul in that he, good old Bert Royal, last of the old-time thief-takers, was putting in his own ticket and following him out of the job. And Vicky? Ah, Vicky, Vicky, he would give her that rusty iron bar from that long-forgotten unsolved murder as a memento of her father in the hope that time would temper her zeal and that one day she would be a better detective than her old man had ever been. His mind made up, Royal swung back towards the Montego, but as he approached the police car he saw that it was empty. Bogan had gone.

Watching Bert Royal pick his way towards the crippled PSU, Bogan was reminded of some pagan rite, the bulbous blue helmets bowed over the sacrifice on the ground, the tableau shrouded in smoke. The eye of the whirlwind had moved on, but he could still hear the dull cries of rioting as his thoughts turned back to Jojo, the silly bitch on the bridge, the carnage in her flat, and then Nigel, taking the dive. He shook his head, trying to dislodge the insect which buzzed in his brain. Nothing made sense.

The itch to be gone became an insistent ache as it dawned upon him that in the police car he was a sitting duck. He got out, sniffed the pungent air, and was about to follow Royal when the shriek of a metal-cutter caught his attention. A fire engine had turned off the road, crossed a strip of open ground and was stopped beside a retaining wall, the cone of its searchlight trained on something hidden from view by the bulk of the machine. The whine of the angle-grinder sang into the night.

Curiosity aroused, Bogan went around the back of the pump escape and stopped, a look of astonishment on his face. The firemen were working on the wreck of a car embedded in the wall, the sleek bonnet crumpled into a concertina of twisted metal, the white hood torn away, yet still instantly recognizable. A smile curled his lip. What d'you know, the yellow Jag had turned up at last! He went up to the fire crew and the Sub-Officer in charge stopped work to greet him.

'Kids these days,' the Sub-O complained, his yellow helmet bobbing, 'what the hell makes 'em tick, I dunno. Car-crazy little bastards, they ought to get an eyeful of this.'

He pointed into the cockpit. The driver was impaled on the steering-wheel, his upper body through the windscreen, his head just mush. The seats had collapsed and the other two were also in the front, rammed into the footwell by the impact, only their legs showing.

'That's what you get when you don't wear your seat-belt,' Bogan observed. 'Instant justice.' As far as he was concerned, the 'hotters' fate was no less than they deserved.

The fireman gave him an odd look. 'How many you count?'

'Three,' Bogan said.

'Four,' the Sub-O corrected him.

'Where?' Bogan cast around, assuming another had been flung out when the Jaguar crashed.

'In the boot.' The fireman grinned, expanding his grisly joke. He was going to enjoy this, the brigade always got the messy jobs, never the cops. 'Want to take a look?'

He led Bogan to the rear of the wreck, the silver XJS marque winking from the undamaged coachwork. The Sub-O released the catch and the boot began to rise. Oh, he was going to enjoy this all right, watch the fat cop chuck his dinner. 'And I tell you something else,' the fireman said. 'He didn't snuff it in the crash either, not unless he chopped himself up and jumped into the bin bags. Be a hard trick to beat.'

Bogan peered into the boot recess. The space was packed with black plastic sacks, seven of them. One had been untied and the Sub-O leaned in and opened it to give him a look inside.

Bogan's stomach heaved. The bag contained a severed head, hair matted, the putty face staring at him, purple tongue lolling from the gaping mouth. He tugged at his tie which was suddenly choking him. The features were familiar as his own, even the scar on the cheek was there, a livid streak across the death mask. No need for a dental chart, he had the picture in his pocket. Bogan gritted his teeth, unable to tear his eyes away. Looking into that face he felt the stone cold chill of certainty. He had found Michael Mitchell.